The Taylor Legacy

An American Family Saga

by

Bert Entwistle

Books by Bert Entwistle

The Drift
Jack Bannister Mystery #1

Uranium Drive-In
Jack Bannister Mystery #2

The Taylor Legacy,
An American Family Saga

New Mexico,
A Novel of the Old West

Leftover Soldiers
Life on the Western Frontier, Book 1

Leftover Soldiers
Aftermath & Opportunity, Book 2

The Black Rose Banker

Murder in the Dell

Looking Back,
Stories of Real American Pioneers

Published in the United States of America by Black Mule Press, Colorado Springs, Colorado 80918
Available from amazon.com, book stores,
and **Black Mule Press:**
<u>email:</u> westernimages@msn.com
<u>phone:</u> **(719) 287-8063**

ISBN# 978-0-9896761-4-4

LOCC: 2016902152

Cover Photo Art © Bert Entwistle

Author Photo: Courtesy of Donald Kallaus

Author's Note

The Taylor Legacy is my fourth novel. My first, *The Drift*, established my detective agency, Black Mule Investigations. My second, *Uranium Drive-In*, took the detectives into another mystery that introduced John Taylor and his Colorado ranching family.

When that published, I sat down in my office and looked around at the surrounding white boards filled with ancestors I had created for this family. I realized I wasn't ready to do away with all these generations of people I had spent so much time with. After a lot of thought, I decided to write about them from the beginning. Burrowing deep into historical research is something I love to do. I often get lost in time while reading about immigrants, coal miners, steamboats, horses, outlaws, and just about anything else that catches my imagination.

This is the story of how the Taylor family of Park County Colorado, came to be. It's really about all of us, who we are and where we came from. This incredible country of ours is a glorious mix of immigrants from every corner of the world. We were founded and settled by people of every color, ethnicity, political philosophy and religion known to mankind. We are all explorers always searching for a better life in our own way. This is the story of one of those families.

For my sons, Jeremy and Chad,

the two best men I've ever known.

The Taylor Family History

"Move only in the moonlight with the star on your shoulder. I hopes God is lookin' over you . . ."

They embraced for a moment, then he left Joe's cabin for the last time.

The Plantation

Charleston, South Carolina
August 8, 1851

The two well-dressed middle-aged men read the newest posting on the door of the sale barn. Dressed in a dove gray silk top-hat and matching vest, Roscoe Dunn peered over his spectacles at the poster.

"Lookin' to buy you a couple more niggers?" asked Abe Peters, his neighbor.

Dunn nodded. "I need new girls for the kitchen and laundry both."

"That all you really want them for?" said Peters, laughing out loud at this. A very fat, unkempt man, he wore an outdated and badly worn beaver hat. His tobacco-stained vest was frayed along the bottom and needed a good cleaning. The two men bit off the ends of their cigars, lit up and headed for the tavern to wait for the sale to start.

Nearly a hundred men had gathered in the sticky midday heat of Charleston. They had surrounded the dock early and waited through the endless business of selling thirty mules and horses of

1

questionable quality. Most were there for the slaves listed on the poster.

Likely and Valuable Slave Sale and Let

Benson & Lockwood
Livestock and Negro Sales

8th of August – 12 noon at the livestock dock

14 Wenches - aged 11 to 51 - two older, near burnouts and two pickaninnys.

17 Bucks - aged 13 to 55 - nine strong hands good for rice work and 8 mixed quality, 3 older, near burnouts and three pickaninnys.

30 horses and mules - to be sold first.

Some credit available to those that qualify

Today's sale was a mixed lot from several different farms, most of them from the Charleston area, and one group brought down from Washington. A common practice in the North was to send unneeded or problem slaves to be sold in the better markets of Charleston. To be *'sold south'* or *'sold down the river'* was the last thing any northern slave ever wanted to hear. Most knew little about escaping to the north, but they knew going south put them even farther away from freedom. Just the thought of it was enough to keep most of them from trying to run.

The auctioneer's assistant, an older local-bred slave known as Pal led the first slave onto the dock, and the chatter from the buyers began to quiet down. The first man to be sold, wore nothing but a ragged pair of pants held up by a short length of rope.

The heavy links of chain connecting his leg irons together made a dull raspy sound as they drug across the rough planks of the platform. The sound was unique. It was one the buyers and sellers had heard many times before.

Barefoot, the rusty iron shackles dug into his ankles and blood trickled down his feet, pooling in the ancient scars in the wood. Before they walked him out, they poured a bucket of water over his head to make him shine in the bright sun.

In many cases, several generations of slave families had made the same walk. The male slaves were also shackled at their wrists with a smaller chain connecting to the lower one.

He looked to be about fifty years old. Unusually heavy for a local slave, he was stoop shouldered, with a pronounced limp and a large swollen lump closing one eye, the likely result of punishment by his overseer. His back showed a long history of the whip.

Working the crowd hard for five minutes the auctioneer failed to raise a single bid. "Okay, tell me what you want done here. You all know how this works; I won't bring out another 'till this one is gone, and I got a whole pen full to get sold today."

Someone in the crowd hollered out, "Two for one, put him with another one."

"Okay. We'll combine this one with lot number two and start again, but I damn well better be hearing some bids."

The second man was younger, around thirty years-old, and very strong looking. The assistant jammed his fingers in the man's mouth and forced it open, declaring him to be in possession of a full set of good teeth, as well as good eyes and ears.

"Now Roscoe," said Peters, "that's a pretty good-looking nigger, don't you think?"

"Could be good in the rice, but what would I do with the old one?"

"Maybe he could work in the harness shop?"

"What if I buy them and you take the old one off my hands for say, a hundred dollars?"

"Jesus Almighty no! He ain't worth the time it'd take to get him home. Plus, it'd cost way too much to feed an old one-eyed pus-gut like him. Whoever gets that one will likely try to sell him for a few dollars or give him away to someone else, he ain't no good for nothin.'"

"You're probably right. I think I'll just wait on the wenches, and maybe a strong young buck to breed to Katty."

"Which one is Katty? I don't remember so well anymore."

"The big fat one in the kitchen, the one that's been helping Moms for a bunch a years."

"Oh yeah, I know her, don't want her for yourself?"

"No, she's got way too fat, besides, you seen her face, all smushed up like it is."

"I know the one, she ain't a pretty thing for sure," said Peters. "She good at makin' suckers?"

"Three girls so far, but I want some bucks, all them girls ain't what I need. That's why I thought a strong young buck might be the answer."

The female slaves were only shackled at the ankles. All had on a long coarse gray skirt and a white shirt that pulled down over their head. If she looked attractive or of breeding age, they stripped off her shirt and lifted her skirt. As the day wore on, Peters spent five-hundred and sixty dollars on one thin, sunken-eyed girl advertised as under twelve.

"I think you got a good one there Abe. Young like that, she should learn quick for sure," said Dunn.

4

"And I'm just the person to learn her. Fact is, I might just learn her some tonight," said Peters. He motioned to Gabe, his oldest most reliable slave to load her in the back of the wagon.

Dunn bought two girls, said to be sisters, both about twelve or thirteen and a fine muscular looking young buck, not much over fifteen or sixteen years old. The buck came from a wheat farm near Washington. He was well over six feet tall and had a pronounced, bullet-shaped head, thick neck, and a much darker color than the girls, just the kind of field worker he liked. In total, he spent $2,250. He locked them to the side board of the wagon while he made a few notes in his sale book.

It was a long trip to the farm. The roads, muddy from last night's storm covered them as they went. The new slaves suffered the ride in silence and there had been no need for the whip.

Dunn and his overseer, Daniel Story, talked about the new slaves and what the girls could be used for. "I think they would be good, one in the laundry and one for Moms," said Daniel. "She's always whinin' about needin' more help."

"What about you Daniel? You ain't had a fresh one for a while."

"Thank you sir, I could use me a fresh one for certain."

"Pick the one you like best. Why don't you and Moms name them, I'm running out of girl names."

"Yessir, what do you want to name the buck?"

"Well, it's August, so call him August, it's as good a name as any."

"He likely had a name from his last place."

"Not anymore."

"Yessir, August it is."

Rounding the last curve, they could see the large arched sign over the entrance announcing the Dunn Rice Company. Two slaves ran out and swung the long gates open for the wagon. For August and the two girls, they would become their own personal gates of hell.

Stopping in front of a low log building, Daniel unlocked the chain holding them together and directed them into the cabin. When they got inside, two older men and one woman, all slaves themselves, began the routine that all new arrivals went through.

Stripping off their clothes, the oldest man, Joe, threw the rags into the fireplace. Next, they were scrubbed with a stiff horsehair brush and lye soap to get off all of the *northern smell,* as Daniel called it, and to remove the lice and whatever else they may have picked up on the way to Charleston.

Child, a slim, middle aged woman born on the farm, did the work on the girls. They had learned years earlier that the new girls were easier to handle if a woman helped them. She bathed them more gently and talked to them in a softer voice which had a calming effect.

They had just been separated from their mother when their owner experienced financial troubles. Their shaking and crying would go on for weeks, sometime months, but the terror in their eyes never went away.

Joe removed the shackles from the girls and Child had them sit on a blanket stretched over a bale of straw. She handed both of them long skirts and shirts that were much too large and a cloth sash for their waist. When they were dressed, she gave them an oversized blue and white scarf along with a pair of crudely made leather shoes. The shoes had no left or right and were all the same large size, but it didn't seem to matter much. Most of them preferred to go barefoot unless they worked in the big house.

August stood naked in the middle of the room with his leg irons still in place, staring straight ahead, silent as a stone. Joe knew from experience this one would be trouble. He carried the familiar look of defiance in his eyes. His muscular body was as tense and hard as oak, and his fists were so tightly clenched they could see the veins pumping through the stretched skin.

They pointed for him to sit on the straw and placed a pair of baggy pants and a button-up shirt on the bale. He got the same shapeless shoes as the girls. He also got a white cloth hat with a wide brim. He didn't move from the middle of the room, never spoke, and continued his distant stare. The two men tried to get him to sit, but he stood anchored to the dirt floor.

Joe found the overseer and told him of the problem. A minute later, Daniel entered the cabin with a whip in his hand. A stout, red-faced, rough looking man, he walked around the new slave and saw immediately that this one would require some special attention. Poking him in the belly with the butt of his whip, he failed to get as much as a sound. Walking behind him, Daniel gave him a brutal kick in the back of the knee and August landed on his back.

As he struggled to his feet, the men pinned him to the ground and threw a rice bag over his head. With two of them holding his body to the ground and the bag covering his face, he lay still. Joe removed his leg irons and slid on his pants. He then put the shoes on the captive and replaced the shackles on his ankles.

The men lifted him to his feet, tied his pants with a piece of rope and pulled off the bag. He resumed his pose, as though nothing had happened. "This buck is gonna have to learn how things work around here, Joe," said Daniel.

"Yessir. He needs to learn, for sure. You wantin' to put his shirt on right now?"

"No, not yet. No need to ruin a perfectly good shirt. Let's see how long he can stand still after gettin' a taste of my leather."

Stepping back a few paces, the overseer let the coils of his leather whip fall to the floor. Made of thin strips of cowhide, the whip was designed especially for this kind of work. Shorter than the ones the teamsters used; it was easier to handle in close conditions. It had a large knob on the end of the handle in case he needed to use it as a club.

He dipped the tail of the whip in the tub of lye water used for the cleaning and jerked it backwards then forwards in one sudden movement. The wet tail hit precisely where he aimed, a skill developed over thousands of lashes given to hundreds of slaves. The leather opened a thin gash from his right shoulder blade, angling down his back nearly to his left hip. Before he could react, the tail of the whip hit him again and left a nearly identical cut an inch from the first one. Blood from the two wounds followed the cuts, running down the left side of his pants. Daniel stood still for a moment, waiting for a response but got nothing.

The cuts, now showing raw muscle and bleeding steadily, began to disappear in a hail of lashes. After thirty strokes, Daniel, now sweating heavily took a long drink of water and went back to work. At forty lashes August began to weaken and dropped to his knees. Five more lashes and he collapsed face down into the bloody dirt.

Now tired and hungry, Daniel took another drink and motioned to Joe and his partner to pick him up. "Put him over the bale and wash him down, then doctor him and put his shirt on. When you're done, lock him up for tonight. We'll finish him up in the morning."

When Daniel left the cabin, Joe and Ned moved him onto the straw and laid him on his stomach. The two men were gentle with him. Having been through all of this themselves, they understood exactly how he felt. They washed him down with clean water and liberally applied salve to his back. The salve was a thick, vile smelling concoction of turpentine and red pepper, mixed with lard to get it to stick together. It was the standard remedy for most slave injuries on the plantation.

*

The next morning, Moms, the kitchen boss, had chosen the girl she wanted and which one would go to the laundry. Her next stop was the harness shop to have Joe make the badges. The shop made the tags as well as taking care of all the harness and blacksmith work. They were square pieces of copper, about two inches wide,

8

with a hole in one corner. On the tag was stamped: *Dunn Rice Co.* Under that were the slave's new names, now called Sara and Ruth, with the date and the job they did. In this case they were both marked *house.* When Moms finished with Sara at night, she would send her to stay with Daniel.

Threading a leather string through the hole, he tied the ends together and placed one over the head of each girl. He also had one made for August, identifying his job as *field.* At the cabin the new slave was sitting up on a straw bale. His hands and feet were still bound, but the chain between them had been removed. The cabin smelled of cornbread and fish, mixed with the powerful odor of the salve and wood smoke. Ned was helping him eat what he could and get down as much water as possible. When he saw Joe come in, he motioned for him to come over. "You have his tag?"

"Yessir, all ready for him. He's to be called August." He put it over his head. "You keep this on always, you understand?" His dark eyes appeared to give a flicker of understanding, then turned away.

"Joe, come close, I want to say something to you, and I don't want no other nigger hearin' us."

"Okay, I's listening."

He pulled him even closer. "This one here, he can speak the language jus' fine. He was a field hand on a wheat farm for a good mas'r up north. He says he jus decided not to talk 'til after he escapes."

Joe leaned closer. "You know mas'r Daniel will whip him bad for not tellin'. You, me and ol' August here, we gots to be quiet around the others."

"I'll be tendin' to him 'til he starts to heal up. I'll let you know what I learn from him, and now we got us a secret — right Joe?"

"We do. I'll try and sneak him a little meat from Moms if I can. He'll need to be gettin' strong so's he can go into the rice." Joe, the oldest slave on the farm, was thought to be somewhere around sixty-five years old. He was born on the same piece of ground he was standing on and had never been farther than Charleston, only a few miles away.

Teaching his new charge about southern plantation life and rice farming proved fairly easy. The two of them understood each other very well, August told him what life was like where he was from and they soon became friends. He was obviously very smart and clearly understood what was happening. After several days, he ended every conversation the same: "I will be whipped by no man — I will escape this place."

Joe hoped he was right, but he told him over and over that talking this way in front of anyone else would surely get him whipped even worse than before — or even killed. He told him how he would need to bide his time and learn the plantation well so he had the best chance of escape when the time came. He also told him to trust no one — white or black.

After the fifth day, Daniel returned to the cabin to check up on his new field worker. Walking in, Joe and August both stood up and faced him. "He's near ready, mas'r," said Joe. "Won't be long now."

The overseer walked over and pulled up his shirt. The scars were mostly scabbed over, with a little pus still seeping from a few of the wounds. The business of whipping new slaves until they bled was normal on many plantations. After the first time, the severity of the lashes could be altered to fit the offense. "He's good to go. Have him at the Split Creek field in the morning. Has he been talking?"

"No talk mas'r, he's a different kind. I think maybe he can't talk, at least not so far."

"Just have him ready for work in the morning."

On their last night together, Joe and August talked about their families, slavery, and freedom. August was determined to escape from here, but he understood the warnings about waiting for the right moment. He would learn the system but he would escape — this much he knew for sure.

The next morning, he was taken to the field by wagon with a dozen other men. As they climbed off the wagon, he remained silent. He wouldn't give the overseer the satisfaction of hearing him speak, at least not yet. He would talk to him when it came time to kill him, and not before.

Escape

August stood knee deep in the muddy flooded rice field. They worked from sunup to sundown, six days a week, exposed to the burning sun and the oppressive humidity of the low country. Mosquitoes swarmed every inch of exposed skin, gorging themselves, often closing his eyes from the swelling. Malaria was a never-ending problem and many slaves and whites had died from the disease.

Daily rainstorms were common. When the sun came out, moisture hung in the still air and wept from the pines and palmettos for hours. When working on dry land, ticks and fire ants found every spot the mosquitoes missed.

Watching the rest of the workers, he was unable to comprehend why everyone was doing this. *Why haven't they escaped?* he wondered. *There are many more of them than there are of the white people.* On his old plantation they were still slaves, but they didn't get treated cruel and they never got whipped. Here they worked in fear of the whip or worse every day.

The driver of the Split Creek field, a slave named Jeps, watched everyone with two sharp eyes and a whip in his hand. His skinny neck and pinched face had gained him the nickname *Rat Driver.* The three slave drivers on the Dunn plantation were charged with ensuring the work was completed and answered directly to the overseer. The overseer monitored the work from horseback, his whip coiled over his shoulder. The slightest offence by the workers could awaken his rage and end in lashes for the guilty party. Slave drivers were hated by the field hands for doing the master's dirty work and generally shunned by the rest of the slave population.

The only relief from the unbearable conditions was in the water. The mud was soft and cool under his feet and he would often submerge himself in the murky water when the driver wasn't looking, washing away the misery of the insects for a brief moment. To be caught would likely mean a few lashes, but Jeps wasn't too sticky on the point if you didn't make it obvious.

He came to the rice fields during the harvest flow. By late summer the fields stayed flooded and the rice was tall. Low country rice fields were a series of dammed up ponds each containing several acres of rice plants irrigated by the brackish water of the local five-foot tides. High tide filled the ponds with water, and a series of wooden gates were closed for as long as the rice needed it. Maintaining the dams and gates was as much work as tending the rice. When they were ready to drain the fields, the gates were opened and the water was drained out at low tide.

This was the first time he'd ever worked rice; he had grown up working wheat. When his owner's farm failed, the slaves were turned over to a teamster and chained together in an open wagon. Then they were transported to Charleston and put on the block.

He had always worked hard where he came from and the work in the rice was no worse. Every day he had food and shelter, and one day a week, the white man's day of rest, he also had a day of rest.

Each slave was given one blanket and one set of clothes plus an extra shirt once a year and a new coat every two years. He was assigned to a cabin in the slave quarter. A crude, swayback shack, it was made of cut tree limbs and scraps of wood. The room was no more than ten by fifteen feet and home to eight workers and three small children. A stone fireplace at one end was used for cooking and heating, and piles of rice sacks filled with straw served as sleeping pallets. Two cast iron cooking pots sat on the hearth and a few cooking items on the mantle.

The floor was made from planks of scrap wood from the plantation's own sawmill. A few cabins had wood floors, but most of the others sat on the dirt. Fuel for the fire was mill scraps and whatever they could scavenge from the forest. A table made from wood planks and two benches were the only furniture. The fine haze of wood smoke mingled with the smell of cooking grease and too many humans in close contact, saturating the cabin and everything in it.

Women without small children worked in the rice alongside the men or in the gardens. They were given a full task to do every day, just like the men. For those with small children, an older woman named Min, chosen because she had outlived her usefulness to the plantation, was assigned to watch the small children. She also took care of the Dunn children. They played together with the black children as though there were no difference. At noon she brought the worker's lunch and the infants to the fields to be fed by their mothers.

August slept against the outer wall pressed against another man named Steven and his wife Lucy. He was fortunate to be able to sleep through their sex and their talking — and the crying. Lucy had a new girl child born with a shriveled leg. Only days old, the baby cried most of the time.

On a Sunday morning the overseer walked unexpectedly into the cabin and saw Lucy feeding her. He noticed the leg immediately. "I heard ye had a new sucker Lucy. Looks like she's all bent up here," he said, poking at the infant's foot with his whip. "She won't be much good for nuthin'. You know what mas'r thinks of such things."

Pulling the blanket over the baby, she looked up at him with terror in her eyes. "Please, sir, please, don't tell him, she won't be no trouble," said Lucy, sobbing uncontrollably.

13

"Not for me to say Lucy. Mas'r decides these things."

August rinsed himself in the tidal water and climbed on the wagon. On the slow ride back to the cabins, the wagon driver asked if anyone was in the cabin with Steven and Lucy. He nodded his head.

"I'm told that Lucy had a girl sucker and mas'r came took her away." *This cannot be true; he would not do this,* thought August. When he reached the cabin, he could hear Lucy wailing before he went inside. She was lying with her head in Steven's lap crying in great heaving sobs. He held her tightly, stroking her head and crying softly to himself.

*

Roscoe Dunn was a third-generation rice farmer. His father, mother, and grandfather all died young and he inherited the farm and more than a hundred slaves when he was twenty-two years old. Ambitious from the start, he promptly went on a search for a wife. He interviewed many local planters and looked at the daughters that were in need of a husband. His choice was a short, plump, pale woman who kept her mousey brown hair pulled back in a severe bun.

Her father, Matthew, owned several large farms bordering on the north side of his and had not yet found a suitable pairing for his daughter. His wife, Beatrice, told him many times he needed to find her a suitor. "She's nearly thirty Matthew. You must find her a husband soon or we will have an old maid on our hands."

Dunn's timing was perfect, if not a bit suspect. Matthew Delany had to provide a much larger dowry than anticipated to get his daughter married off to a well-to-do area planter.

Margaret Clarice Delany, daughter of wealthy planter, Matthew Fitzpatrick Delany and wife Beatrice Eve, became Mrs. Roscoe Dunn on a hot summer day in June of 1853. Her father paid for everything, including the most expensive dress in Charleston.

When the wedding day arrived, slaves attended to her needs and set up the house for more than fifty guests. Dishes of beef, pork and chicken lined the side boards along one wall of the dining room and fresh vegetables and desserts lined the other side. Arrangements of fresh picked flowers sat between the different dishes. The table was set with four different wines and the third generation Delany family silver.

When the ceremony was over the guests watched as she opened the gifts. Roscoe sat on a chair to one side of his bride, nodding and smiling as she showed him each item. Motioning to one of the house slaves she pointed to the gifts. "Take these to the study and prepare them to be boxed and put in the carriage. And there will be hell to pay if you break anything! Understand?"

Beatrice leaned close to Matthew's ear. "Good luck to Roscoe Dunn with this one . . ."

Matthew nodded. "Good luck indeed."

Margaret took over control of the Dunn house, its slaves, and all domestic business within days of her arrival. By the end of the month she had everything running the way she wanted it. The new lady of the house commanded attention wherever she went and ran the house like a general ran his army. To disrespect her would often bring swift and severe punishment.

She complained to Roscoe how hard it was to get the house slaves to do what she wanted. "I never understood why my mother had so much trouble with her house niggers. Now I know why; they are lazy and arrogant. Why can't they learn to read and write? Do you know how much work it would save if they could write things down?"

"Now Margaret," said Roscoe, looking over the top of his paper, "we've talked about this before. Moms has been with the family for twenty years. If you'd just tell her what you want, she'll take care of it. She doesn't like change. Besides, it's against the law to teach the blacks to read and write, you know that. It will just take a little time and the two of you will get along just fine."

"She's just lazy! I'll give her a little time, but I promise you, she *will* do it my way."

*

Walking into the roadhouse, Roscoe spied several local planters sitting at a corner table. He ordered a rum and sat down next to Abe Peters. "Roscoe, how's the new niggers working out?"

"Moms says the girls are okay. The buck seems to be botherin' Daniel some though. Says he don't talk one bit; thinks he might be a mute."

"That can't be all bad, long as he works hard and maybe breeds up a couple of boy suckers."

"I suppose that's so. They say he works hard in the rice and he could be a good breeder. Daniel says that he noticed him keepin' time with a daughter of Moms. A pretty, fair-skinned mulatto with soft hair called Sally."

"Soft hair? Now where do you think that soft hair and fair skin come from?" said Abe. Of all the local planters, Peters was the crudest Roscoe had ever met. He had no wife or family and ran a shabby, rundown rice operation. He lived for young slave girls and used the whip for any infraction of the rules. Even his overseer left him more than a year ago.

"No idea Abe."

Many slave owners in the area had mulatto children on their farm. It was a common practice but most owners chose not to talk about it so publicly. As a plantation owner, Roscoe was more inclined to let the overseer run the day to day operation. As long as things were profitable and Margaret was happy, he didn't get too involved, and he didn't really like to talk about it with people like Abe. Margaret called him a smelly twisted old man, and hated it when he brought him home.

"You thinkin' of sellin' her?"

"Sally? No, I ain't gonna sell her. She could be makin' me a strong rice hand right now."

16

The men talked business, drank rum, and told stories for several hours. The other planters had already left the tavern, but Roscoe and Abe chose to stay and drink. By one in the morning, the rum had done its work and neither could walk on their own. Peters motioned to Gabe who had been waiting on a stool in the corner. "Okay, it's time. Load me up and take me home."

Gabe helped his master up and steered him toward the door, the wagon was already waiting outside. "Roscoe, you better let Gabe take you home too . . ."

"You could be right about that. Otherwise, I'll be sleepin' here tonight," said Dunn, trying to keep himself from falling from his chair.

After several years of marriage, Margaret Dunn had accepted the drinking and the late-night return of her husband passed out in a wagon. If a fondness for rum was the worst she could expect from him, she could live with it. Pregnant with their third child, she had more important things to do than babysit a drunk. Her time and energy went into running the house and keeping her slaves in line. Soon there would be a new baby and she needed to find the right slave to care for it.

*

It was Sunday morning and Margaret shooed her husband outside. "Go down to the quarter and start looking for a pair of wenches that can take care of this baby. I don't want any that are lazy or talk back — understand?"

Roscoe's head was crashing from last night's rum. The thought of getting away from her for a while might be a good idea. Finding Daniel, they walked toward the quarter. "Got any thoughts on a couple of baby nurses?"

"Well, there are a couple mas'r. Moms' second girl, Sally, seems to be good with all the little kids. She's about the right age and don't got no suckers of her own. There's Mary, she's from one of the tree cutters you sold last year. She's maybe fourteen years or so."

The big house was set back from the slave quarter separated by a thin stand of pines. From the front porch you could only see a long, grassy pasture with cows grazing. Off the back of the house was the cook shack and the laundry connected to the back door by a short path. Moms and the laundry workers stayed in the back.

Built in a style common to the area, the big house was seventy-three years old, two-stories, with tall columns and a long balcony. The house was completely whitewashed, with large green shutters and surrounded by several enormous moss-covered live oaks. It looked the part of a successful southern planter's home. A road curved up to the front porch and plantings of dogwood and honeysuckle graced either side of the front steps. Blue indigo flowers ran below the rest of the porch.

Like most local planters' homes, the facade concealed what it took to keep a plantation like this operating. Margaret managed twenty slaves that did the cooking, cleaning, child care, laundry, gardening, and valet work. The family lived on the second floor with two small rooms set aside for the body servants and nurses. The first floor was for the dining room and other common areas, as well as quarters for the house servants.

As the two men walked past the pines, the real heart of the Dunn Rice Company came into view. The slave quarter was a long clearing, cut into the trees with two rows of eight cabins facing each other. They backed up to the tree line and the space between the rows was nearly fifty yards wide and completely taken up by vegetable gardens. A dozen women worked at picking beets, cabbage, okra, carrots, and greens of all kinds. The fresh food was taken first to the kitchen for Moms to use in the big house, and the excess divided up among the slaves. Any extra food not used on the plantation was allowed to be used by the slaves or sold to travelers and guests for extra money.

At the end of the rows facing the garden sat a slightly larger cabin, this one for the overseer. Behind the cabin, scattered through the trees were several more structures. The sawmill was the largest, then the carriage house, blacksmith, and harness shop. Hog pens, as well as a butcher house, smokehouse and milking shed each had their own building. There were several others for storage and a shed used to winnow the rice.

The plantation was a city in itself, a self-sustaining operation of nearly two hundred people. The only whites were the members of the family and the overseer. Roscoe always liked the scene when he came around the trees, to him it meant success. The Dunn Rice Company had made a profit in thirty-seven of the last forty years and he planned on continuing the tradition.

Walking alongside the gardens, he stopped at a bare post buried in the ground, sticking up eight feet in the air. The post was in clear view of the cabins, set there for that reason. It held up the slave that was being punished at the time. "You had to use it lately Daniel?"

"I did mas'r. Couple of 'em caught stealing out of the garden, and once on August jus' a few days ago. You remember him, mas'r? The one that don't talk?"

"For what reason was he whipped?"

"For refusin' a work order. I caught him and Sally sneakin' into the woods when they shoulda' been startin' work."

He mulled this over for a minute. "Are they in the same field?"

"Yessir, they are."

"Did you punish Sally too?"

"Not yet mas'r, I was waitin' to speak with you first."

"Take me to her."

She was sitting with August on a bench in front of his cabin when they walked up. "Sally, Missus Dunn wants a new nurse for when the baby gets here," said Roscoe. "She will be ready for you in a few weeks. You will live in the big house and care for her and the child. Understand?"

"Yessir mas'r. I understand."

"Did you go into the woods when you were supposed to be in the rice?"

"Yessir, mas'r."

"Fifteen strokes. And Daniel, don't cut her bad. I want her healed before she goes to the house."

"Yessir mas'r. Fifteen strokes."

"Now take me to Mary."

Sally, now crying softly was comforted by August. Alone in the cabin, they sat down on their pallet. "If I go to the big house, we can't be together . . ."

Neither had ever been in the big house before, but they knew the chances of them being together after she became a nurse were nearly impossible. When August first came to the plantation, he knew after the first whipping he would escape. After several years of backbreaking work and enduring more whippings, he felt ready to go.

Before he had made a plan to escape, he met Sally. He'd seen her before, at Sunday prayers and other occasions. They had looked at each other several times, once brushing shoulders as they worked in the garden. Another time, after the Sunday prayers she walked right up to him and touched him on the arm. He turned to see who it was. She was looking up into his eyes and smiling. "August, I'm Sally."

Slim and delicate, she was light skinned and very pretty. From that moment forward they were together every chance they had. They were in each other's arms every day, even if it meant sneaking away and risking Daniel's leather.

Sally held him tightly, sobbing softly, not wanting to let go. "I can't do it. I'm scared 'bout the whip and I'm scared 'bout the big house."

August brushed away her tears. "No one will ever hurt you; I promise. He won't whip you today. Mas'r don't like punishin' on Sunday."

Sally, still holding him tight, spoke quietly to him. "August, I am with child."

He kissed her gently. He had been on the farm more than four years, much longer than he had intended. "Then we will start tonight. I must talk to old Joe first, then we will get ready."

*

"You know the north star good?" asked Joe.

"Yessir, you taught me well."

"You remember the name of the town?"

"Yessir, I remember."

"You remember the other names I gave you?"

"I remember."

"You and Sally goin' together?"

"We are."

"August, you know you can't never come back here, ever. You know what they will do if they catch you . . ."

"I do. I have a little food, a blanket and my knife."

"Move only in the moonlight with the star on your shoulder. I hopes God is lookin' over you," said Joe. They embraced for a moment, then he left Joe's cabin for the last time.

When the hour was late and the quarter quiet, he slipped silently out of his cabin and into the woods. Walking slowly through the damp pines, his bare feet found the quietest spots to step. Reaching the overseer's cabin, he looked through the window and saw Daniel in the dim light of the fire, asleep on his pallet.

Stepping inside, he stood directly over him for several minutes, staring at his tormenter. "Evenin' mas'r Daniel, time to wake up now. I gots somethin' for you."

Daniel rolled over and looked up at him. "Who the hell is doin' all this talkin' and wakin' me in the middle of the night?"

"It's me mas'r, August. Your favored whippin' nigger . . ."

"August don't speak, you can't be him . . ."

"Wrong, mas'r, I am August and I speak good."

The overseer's mind raced. "Why are you here? Is this because of Sally?"

"No," he said, now holding a rice knife in his hand. "It's about you and me. You will never whip me or anyone else ever again."

As the overseer pulled himself up, August swung the curved blade, slicing open the left side of his neck.

Grabbing at his neck to stop the blood flow he tried to get up again. "You goddamned animal — I'm gonna kill you!"

Swinging the knife again, he sliced through the right side of his neck. Falling back on the pallet, Daniel made a soft gurgling sound, blowing a fine bloody mist from his mouth.

August stood over him, watching the last of his life drain away. "No one will whip me ever again — no one."

*

Roscoe stood on his porch in the early morning light drinking his tea and watching the slaves move into the fields. He heard Jeps let out a loud cry. "Two niggers gone mas'r! Two niggers gone!"

"Two gone? Where the hell is Daniel this morning?"

"Don't know mas'r, he not here yet."

"Who is it that's missing?"

"August and Sally mas'r, not in the cabin this morning."

"Goddamnit to hell," screamed Dunn, now red in the face. "Get my carriage, and get the dogs ready."

Within minutes Jeps and Dog Boy had a dozen hounds straining at the leash waiting for instructions. "Take them to their cabin and start there. They should be able to pick up the scent pretty easy. I'm going to look for Daniel. Put everyone back in the quarter 'til I figure out what's going on."

The scene in the overseer's cabin sickened him and shattered his fragile sense of plantation security. Daniel lay on his back with his neck cut almost through. The curved rice knife was buried deeply in his chest and blood soaked everything in the cabin. In the fire were the remains of his whip, now reduced to embers.

Jeps and Dog Boy started at August's cabin, giving the dogs a shirt thought to belong to August. The barking hounds milled around the cabin for half an hour before the two men finally got them started into the woods. The dogs put their noses to the ground and led them right to the overseer's cabin. "Guess we know who killed Daniel," said Jeps. "Now we gots to find him."

After the dogs were turned loose in the woods, he rode for Charleston and hired two slave hunters. With the deal made, they all headed out to catch up with the dogs before they got too far away. "You can count on them heading for the coast. They will likely try and get on a ship," said the slave hunter. "Niggers ain't all that smart Mr. Dunn. You get some posters up in the area quick and put on a reward. That way, if we don't catch up to them right away, someone up there will grab them."

For three days, the slave hunters and dogs scoured the countryside looking for any sign of the missing slaves. Posters describing the pair as escapees and murderers were hung all over the Charleston coastal area. They described them as a young, strong buck, six feet and mute, named August, and a fair-skinned mulatto called Sally. A seven-hundred-and fifty-dollar reward was offered for each of them for their live return. By the fourth day they had a few tips from those looking for some reward money, none of which proved to be of any value.

At the plantation, life was returning to its normal stifling routine. Dunn had hired a new overseer, a man with a reputation even worse than Daniel's. Several slaves had been interrogated and whipped looking for information, but the quarter had nothing to say about the missing pair. Even if they knew anything, the overseer knew he would never get them to talk. The slave hunters were on the path north up the coast, confident they could find them. Dunn could do nothing but wait and hope they got his property back.

*

Seven days after the murder, late on a dark night when the quarter was asleep, Steven and Lucy pried up two planks from the floor of the cabin and helped Sally and August climb out of their hiding place. The two men had dug out the space below the floor over the

23

last year, carrying the dirt to the rice fields and the garden every day a little at a time. After a year of work, they had a space as long as a man and deep enough to sit up in. It was just wide enough to hold two people and a few supplies. If August and Sally were successful, Steven and Lucy would be the next to try.

Slipping silently into the trees, the two fugitives disappeared from the plantation into the night. They walked quietly for several hours in the cool darkness. "August, how do you know which way to go?"

Stopping for a rest at the edge of a small stream, he put his arm around her and wrapped her in his blanket. "Joe showed me 'bout the North Star and how to tell what the directions are if you're lookin' right at it."

"How's that gonna help us?"

"The star is the north direction," he said, pointing it out to her. "Joe says that most runaways try and go straight north or sneak up the coast line. It's the shortest route to the free state."

"Are we goin' that way too?"

"No, we goin' to the west direction, it's longer, but they won't be lookin' for us that way."

"How does the star help us then?"

"We keep the North Star lookin' down on our right shoulder. We walk at night and hide during the day. When the stars come out, we start walkin' again."

Macon

August held Sally tight to him, using his coat to cover her from the sudden rain. After more than twenty nights of travel they had begun to fall into a routine. Keeping to the thickest trees and close to water when they could, was safer and easier to get food. They found a large piece of canvas in an abandoned barn to use for shelter and to sleep on. In another spot he entered the root cellar of a local farm and took two jars of potatoes. They added this to their meager supply of rice and hush puppies. Several times he took from local cellars, taking only what they needed and no more.

As soon as the skies began to lighten, they would be deep in the woods under a fallen tree or in some thick brush huddled under the canvas for the remainder of the day. Twice people rode by close enough to see them if they hadn't been so well concealed. Both times the horses had clearly picked up their scent but the riders never noticed. Each time he gripped the handle of the long butcher knife he had taken from the overseer's cabin, ready to use it if needed.

Cattle and sheep often grazed nearby and more than one rabbit or squirrel was startled to find themself huddled in the same brush pile. Dogs were a problem, and more than once they sacrificed a bit of their precious food to quiet one down. Once a stubby black mongrel followed them for two days. When he realized they had no more food he disappeared. Another day was spent burrowed into a large haystack, while a farmer plowed in the next field. They talked about their future and made love under the canvas. He was still amazed he had found this beautiful girl. Most of the time on the plantation, he never even thought about women. Since he met Sally, she was all he could think of.

When the last of the daylight disappeared, they rolled up their possessions in the canvas, checked for the North Star and started to walk. On several nights, spring storms moved into the area concealing the star. When it wasn't visible, they huddled together in the thickest part of the forest they could find to wait out the day.

They were constantly wet. One-night Sally began to shake uncontrollably. "August, I am so cold, we must get warm somehow."

"We have to keep moving, it will help us stay warm. We will look for dry shelter as we go. After several more hours of walking, he looked across an open field and saw an orange glow and a thin swirl of smoke floating above the trees. As they moved closer, they saw a large pile of trees and brush burning from a recently cleared field.

"Not likely to be anyone tending this burn so late at night. We can get warm for now and get back in the trees when it gets light," said August.

Stepping as close as they dared, they stripped off their wet clothes and waved them back and forth over the fire. For the first time in days they were warm, dry, and felt like they could keep going. After they dressed, August rolled everything else into the canvas, set it aside and hugged Sally. "Here, have some rice, you need to eat something."

Sally nodded and took the food. "I love you August, I know that we will be good now."

"I love you too." Staring at the burning brush pile he realized that they weren't alone. A single figure stood silhouetted against the fire. He was wearing a floppy hat and carried a shovel over his shoulder. They stood staring at each other, each waiting to see what the other would do.

August stepped in front of Sally and showed the stranger his empty hands. "Sir, we mean no harm; we're just getting warm. We will leave now."

The stranger walked closer to him. "Don't go. I am just here to watch over the fire. I'm Seth. I belong to the master of this farm. He's gone to the city for a few days and there's only me to watch the place. Are you hungry?"

"We don't want to bother you none," said August. "We'll just leave you alone."

"Nonsense. Come with me and have something to eat. I want to hear about your journey."

August looked at Sally and she nodded her approval. "Thank you Seth, but you can understand why we are so careful about these things."

"I do. I escaped once, but they caught me and brought me back. I still carry the scars from it."

Following him through the trees, they came to a cabin just large enough for three or four people. "Sit by the fire, I have some fresh rabbit stew."

After the meal, they told Seth about the rice farm and their escape, leaving out the part about the murder. "We are travelling to a town in the West called Macon, have you ever been there?"

Seth shook his head. "Don't know it. I never leave this place." They talked for a long time, telling each other about their history and their owners. When the conversation died down, they all fell asleep in front of the fireplace.

August woke up and realized it was daylight and they were not yet in the woods. He quickly woke up Sally. Seth was nowhere to be seen. He considered what to do next. There was no window and he didn't want to open the door and risk being seen.

While they were talking about it, the door opened and Seth walked in. "Good morning friends. I was just checking the fire and getting fresh water."

"Seth, we slept too long," said August. "Now we have to get to the woods without anyone seeing us."

"I understand. But if you stay here, you will be safe. I will take you to the woods tonight."

27

They didn't want to lose a day of travel, but one more day of rest would be a good thing.

Sally nodded. "Thank you Seth, we would like to stay today and leave tonight."

When the stars were bright enough, Seth showed them to a faint trail in the trees. "This runs mostly to the west. Good luck my friends."

August found the North Star and shook Seth's hand. "Thank you for everything and take care."

After a month of close calls and cold damp nights, they reached the banks of the Ocmulgee River just below Macon. He told Sally that Joe said he needed to remember three things. The river was the first name he gave him. "Then, follow the river north until you come to the town of Macon." The third name was of a man called Davis, who worked for a white planter on the north bank of the river, several miles above town.

The planter lived in a large, two story log house with white double-doors in the front, and had another smaller cabin that sat back in the trees. "That is the one where Davis lives," Joe had told him. "He will help you from there. Just remember to approach his cabin from the trees at night so nobody sees you." "Has Joe been here before?" asked Sally.

"Joe ain't never been off the plantation 'cept to town a few times."

"Then how does he know about this place?"

"Don't really know, he just does."

*

Peering out from under the canvas and through the brush he could see a faint flickering light through a tiny window in the back of the cabin. After several hours of darkness, he decided to approach it. This was the scariest moment of the trip, because he could not know what would happen when he tapped on the door.

Standing in front of the door, he gathered up his courage and tapped three times. The door opened slightly. "You alone?"

"I have my wife."

"Get her in here quickly and quietly," said the stranger.

He motioned to Sally and in a moment, they were inside the cabin. Warmth from the fire engulfed them for the first time in weeks. "You be Mister Davis?"

"Just Davis, and you are?"

"I am August and this is Sally, she is with child."

"Excuse me for not lighting a lamp. I don't want anything to appear unusual in the middle of the night. Have a seat in front of the fire and warm yourself. Here are some blankets. This is my wife Mae; she will give you something to eat. You are hungry I assume?"

"We are, thank you." After the meal he told them to get some sleep and he would explain everything in the morning.

They awoke to find the cabin very warm and Mae cooking a breakfast meal. He realized that two small faces, a boy about twelve and a girl several years younger, were sitting on a pallet in the corner. He hadn't seen them the night before.

"Are we close to the free state?" asked Sally.

"No, you still have a ways to go," said Mae.

"Stay in the cabin and keep warm," said Davis. "I will be back in a while." Mae brought them a tin plate with stew and bread. "Eat good, there's plenty to go around."

After the meal, they thanked her and asked if there's anything they could do to help. "Not yet, thank you. When he gets done talking with mas'r, he will tell you then."

August tensed up. "He's telling your mas'r about us? No — this cannot be . . . Joe told me we were safe here."

"It's okay, not to worry none. You are safe. This mas'r is a conductor, he helps people like us."

"What is a conductor?"

"A conductor helps people on the railroad get to where they goin'."

"Your mas'r work for the railroad people? Are we goin' on a railroad train?"

"Just don't you worry. You stay by the fire and keep warm. He will tell you 'bout it when he get back. Mister August, how is old Joe doing?"

He was surprised to hear her ask about the old man. "How is it that you know Joe?"

"I was born on the Dunn Plantation a long time ago. When I was a young girl, I was taken from my momma and sold to a man in Atlanta as a house slave. He were a filthy old man that died after a year or so. Then I was sold to another man on an indigo farm. When the farm went bad, I was sold at auction to this mas'r. Been with him ever since. It's all for the better here for sure."

"Well, Joe is good. He's the one that told us to come here. Now I know why."

The door opened and Davis walked in with a tall straight white man about seventy years old. He had frizzy white hair and a scruff of a beard and very long sideburns. He also had the most piercing blue eyes they had ever seen. "My name is Angus Drummond; did Davis tell you anything about me?"

"No sir, he just said not to worry, that you won't turn us in."

"He's right. We're all going to help you get to the free state of Illinois. When you get there, someone else will be waiting to help you to the next stop."

"Sally and me thank you sir, but we have nothing to pay you with."

"We need no payment; this is our job, me and Davis. We help black people escape from slave owners. That's what we do."

He thought about this revelation for a while. A white man and a black man working together to help slaves escape was nothing he'd ever heard of before. "Sir, how you plan on gettin' us there without the slave hunters catchin' us?"

"Why, we're going down the road just like everyone else does, right down the middle of it," said Drummond. "Then we're going

30

to take a nice boat ride all the way to your freedom. What do you think of that?"

August was confused as to how that could be, but nodded his head. "Sir, I never heard of such a thing before, but me and Sally are ready to see the free state."

Drummond asked her to stand up. "Miss Sally, you are a very pretty girl. Your light skin will be the secret to us getting safely to Illinois. I will be your uncle and you will become my niece by my sister in Chicago."

"Sir," said Sally. "You think I could pass for a white girl? That sounds very dangerous for all of us."

"Don't worry. When Mae is through fixing you up, even August wouldn't know you."

When the old man left, August was full of questions for Davis. "Are you sure about this? Has this ever been done before? How will Sally look like a white girl? What about me? Why does he do this?"

Davis assured him that his mas'r knew exactly what he was doing. "He has helped forty people escape. His family lived in Virginia; they were small farmers near a place called Leesburg. They were attacked by two southern men, and his brother and two sisters were killed. They owned no slaves and had been publicly speaking out against it for years. He has been helping us ever since."

"Are you a slave?"

"He bought me and Mae at an auction in Atlanta many years ago. When we got back to the farm, he sat us down and told us about what he was doing and said he would give us our freedom. Then he asked if we would think about helping him on his mission."

"How long you been here?"

"Something over ten years now I think. He gave us our freedom right away, like he said he would. But he is such a good man that we are comfortable here and want for nothing so we stay and we help with his mission."

Sally had been listening intently to his story. "Mister Davis, is there a Missus Drummond?"

"No, she died several years ago. He misses her something terrible. Afterward it made him work even harder for us."

*

After two days they were healed up from the trip and had eaten all they could. Mae took Sally aside and showed her what she needed to do for the trip. She was given fresh clothes and a hat with a wide brim and a black veil. "You will be wearing these for the trip. You need to look like a proper young white woman. Each morning you will wash your face and dry it good, then you will put on a very thin cover of this white powder, just a little. I will show you how when you are ready to leave."

August wondered about all this preparation and the new clothes for Sally. He'd never seen anyone dressed up like this. She looked more beautiful than ever. The next morning Drummond came to the cabin and sat down next to them. "August, you need to know how to drive a two-horse buggy. Can you do that?"

"Yessir, I did that for my first mas'r. I worked all his horses for him."

"Good. Tomorrow morning we will be off for Atlanta. Now listen closely, these are the parts you will have to play. I am a wealthy farmer and am accompanying my niece, Sally Henson, back home to Cairo, in southern Illinois. Sally, you just received word that your mother Mary passed away. Can you do this?"

"I can do it Mister Drummond; I can do it easy."

"What about my part," asked August.

"You have the most difficult part. It will be hard on you from the time we leave."

"Whatever it is, I can do it."

"I'm sure you can. You will be the driver. You will drive and switch the horses and care for them when we stop." Drummond paused for a moment. "Until we get to Illinois you will be my nigger, you will be treated like people expect a slave to be treated. Do you understand what I'm saying?"

"I think so. I need to be actin' like I was still on the plantation and I was afraid of the whip."

"That's exactly right. You must behave by following every order I give you. Even if you don't understand it or like it, you have to act like you know you will get the leather if you don't. I may yell and curse you and treat you poorly. It's what the white people are used to seeing," said Drummond. "We can't let anyone see that you know Sally, and we can't let anyone know that we look at you as anything but a common slave."

"I understand sir. If that's what it takes to be free, I will be the perfect slave."

"You have to call me mas'r from now until we're there. You have to remember your parts."

It was a lot for August to readily accept, but if Davis said it's so he would do it. "Yessir mas'r."

Just before the sun came up, Davis pulled in front of the cabin in a new black buggy. Tying off the reins, he motioned for August and Sally to come out. Davis lifted her small trunk into the carriage just as Drummond appeared with his own slightly larger trunk and a thick cane with a large silver head in the shape of a bear. After they were loaded, Sally and Angus, both dressed as wealthy family members, climbed in the back and pulled down the side curtains. August untied the horses, climbed into the driver's seat and snapped the reins

As the sun warmed the buggy, they lifted the side curtains and tied them up. "This is my brand-new Amesbury Carriage Company buggy," said Drummond. "They build some of the best carriages in the country. I had it custom built to my specifications. It just arrived two weeks ago. Do you feel how soft these seats are?"

"Yessir, they're very comfortable, sir."

"Sally, you need to call me uncle, or Uncle Angus, not sir, remember?"

"Yes uncle, I remember now."

"Good. I had the buggy made with better springs, wider wheels and tires and axles that are heavier than normal. The roads can be very bad between here and Atlanta and we want the best ride we can get, especially for an old man like me."

"It is very nice uncle. I have never been in anything like this before."

"Time to put your veil down girl. We will be going through town and don't want anyone to see your face too clearly."

August proved to be a good driver and horseman, changing horses at the first stop without a problem. While Angus and Sally refreshed themselves at the roadhouse he sat on the driver's seat and waited. When they came out of the roadhouse, he, untied the horse and opened the door for them. "Here boy, here's something to eat."

He unwrapped the paper and found a boiled potato and a piece of cooked beef. Pulling back onto the road, he ate while he drove. They stopped a second time to change horses about halfway to Atlanta. The third time they stopped was a repeat of the first time. Angus and Sally went into the roadhouse, a squat, crude-looking log building full of rough-looking men and sat near the single window. The inside smelled heavily of wood smoke. A stout, middle-aged woman with a greasy towel around her waist and another one over her shoulder addressed them.

"What do you want today?"

Angus told her he wanted a pint of ale and a mug of water for his niece, "and some bread and steak for three if you have it."

"We have it, why for three?"

"One for my niece, one for me and one for my nigger, is there a problem?

"No problem sir. Shall I wrap the one for the nigger?"

34

"Yes, in fact, wrap all three of them — and hurry up," said Drummond, looking over the men in the room.

Finishing his ale, they walked out the door toward the buggy. When they got outside, he saw August backed up against the buggy by two rough looking men. The shorter of the two was poking him in the chest with his finger. "Boy, where's your master? Did he forget you? Look here Bob, I think we got us a free nigger. I bet he'll bring a couple hundred at the sale barn."

Before he could say anything else, Drummond brought down the silver head of his cane onto the stranger's right hand with a vicious blow, causing him to scream out loud and jump back several feet. Drummond towered over the man by half a foot and his blue eyes locked instantly on the stranger. "You're trying to steal my property? You sir are nothing but a common thief and I will march you to the local authorities right now . . ."

"Mister, I wasn't stealing him. I was just havin' a little fun with him."

Bringing down the cane a second time, he hit him again in the same hand. The man screamed again and looked at his hand. "Goddamnit you old bastard, my hand is broke! You're gonna pay for this, you son of a bitch!" Reaching under his coat with his other hand, he grabbed for a knife. In an instant he heard a metallic click against his forehead. Drummond pressed a cocked pistol firmly against his head.

"Stranger, you really need to learn some proper manners. Now give me the knife, handle first," said Drummond. Tossing it into the buggy, he motioned for Sally and August to get in. "I'm going to be on my way now. If I ever see you near my boy again, I will put a nice round hole in your head. Is there anything I just said that you don't understand?"

Shaking his head, the stranger backed up, holding his hand cradled to his chest. "I understand."

"Good, now get the hell out of my sight."

Boats and Trains

Reaching Atlanta, the travelers stopped for the night at a large modern roadhouse called the Burgan Hotel. A solid red brick structure, three stories high with tall white columns on either side of the entrance. It was the place to stay for those who could afford it. Drummond used it whenever he was in town, and he was well known by everyone there. It served meals and drinks and provided a dozen rooms for travelers. In the back was a horse barn that had been closed in on one end with a sign over the door that read **BLACKS**, with a row of sleeping grain sack pallets and a fireplace at one end.

After Drummond and Sally had their supper, she retired to her room and he brought a meal out to August. Walking into the barn, the damp acrid smell of manure hit him when he stepped through the door. He saw August wiping down the buggy. "Boy, here's some food. Remember what I told you last time. Keep those seats brushed clean as a whistle or you're lookin' at the leather again, you hear me?"

"Yessir mas'r, I hear you."

Drummond walked past several other black men who had been listening to the conversation. "What the hell are you lookin' at? Niggers without something to do ain't nothin' but trouble. You want me to fetch your masters?"

The men all lowered their heads and moved away, suddenly finding something to occupy them. When he was gone, one of the men asked August, "Is it true? Does he whip you?"

He nodded and pulled up his shirt for them to see. "This is what happens when he gets mad or too drunk."

"Did you ever try to escape?"

36

"Once. After he whipped me, he said he would kill me if I did it again and I believe him."

Drummond walked back to the roadhouse with a slight bit of a smile. His room was next to Sally's and he knocked quietly on the door. "This is Uncle Angus, are you all right for the evening?" "I'm fine uncle, thank you. I'm just very tired from the ride."

"Goodnight then. Just knock on my door if you need anything, anything at all."

*

Leaving Atlanta, they had over a hundred miles to go to reach Chattanooga. They passed through the city early in the morning through a maze of railroads and the haze of steam engines belching out choking black smoke. The roads were rough and the recent rain had turned some areas into thick mud. They soon covered enough distance to reach fresh air for the first time since they arrived.

The first two days out of Atlanta were wet and windy, but Drummond's custom buggy kept them dry and relatively warm. August continued to drive the buggy without complaint, wearing his extra coat and his hat pulled down low. At the halfway point, the weather cleared and they put up the curtains.

"August," said Drummond, "pull over by this little stream so we can take a break."

When the buggy stopped, he helped Sally down. Walking to the stream he bent down for a drink. After some jerky and bread, Drummond told them they had been doing good so far, but the journey would get worse before it got better. "The closer we get to a free state; the more suspicious people get. Slave hunters are everywhere. We must be extra vigilant from now on."

After another night at a roadhouse and a long day's ride, they arrived in Chattanooga, along the banks of the Tennessee River. Drummond directed August to a dirt road south of town and onto a long twisting lane disappearing into the trees. The farmhouse was surrounded by cotton fields. The buggy pulled directly into the barn and a black man appeared to close the doors behind them. "Mister Mills is waiting for you in the house," said the man as he tied up the horse. "I'll take you there."

Inside the house, Mason Mills directed the travelers to chairs in front of the fireplace. "I'm glad you made it, Angus, any trouble on the road?"

"No more than usual, a couple of men that talked tough, though they proved not to be."

"These are our passengers I take it?" asked Mills.

Drummond nodded. "This is Sally and August, most recently from the Dunn Rice Plantation near Charleston."

At that moment, a stately, middle-aged woman entered the room with a tray of bread and cheese and several pieces of ham. "I'm Jewel, Mason's wife. We're glad you made it here safely. You can rest with us for a day or two and then ready yourselves for the next part of the trip."

"Mister Mills, is the man in the barn a slave?" asked August.

"No, though I understand why you might ask that question. Ben is my employee. I have several black people who work for me," said Mills. "They are all freed slaves who help me with this operation. They carry their manumission papers and a letter from me at all times. They choose to stay and help me on the farm and help with the escaped slaves. We pay them and take good care of them while they're here. Any time they're ready to move on, they will take the same trip you're about to."

Jewel showed them to a small room just wide enough and long enough for two people. A pallet and a stack of blankets were all that were in the windowless space. The door was under the stairwell, well-hidden by furniture. "We still need to be careful. The slave hunters are relentless. They will grab any black person they can find if they think they can make a dollar. You will need to stay here until you're ready to go."

*

The next morning Sally and August joined them at the table. The curtains were drawn and the room was dark except for a pair of oil lamps on the table and the glow of the fireplace. "Here's what will happen on the next part of the trip," said Drummond. "Mister Mills and I are the owners of a steamboat called *The Belle of Rochelle.* We make our money in the cotton business. I grow it and he ships it as well as freight from other people too. That's how we afford to do these kinds of things."

"Are we going to ride on a steamboat uncle?" asked Sally.

"You and August are taking the next leg of the trip on the *Belle,* along with tons of cotton and other cargo."

"Where will the steamboat take us?"

"You will get to a town called Cairo, in the state of Illinois. Then you will transfer to another conductor."

"Is this state of Illinois a free state?" asked August. "Will we be free then?"

"Illinois is a free state, but you must keep moving North. If you stay there, it would be too easy for the slave hunters to find you and take you back."

"Will I be driving a buggy again?" asked August.

"That will be up to the next conductor. He will do what's best for you at the time."

"We are ready to be free," said August, squeezing Sally's hand. "We want our child to be born free."

"In preparation for the trip, there are a few things you need to carry with you." Mills gave both of them a small leather pouch with a string to hang it around their neck. "This is to hold your papers and money. Keep it around your neck under your clothes. This is very important. Never take it off or show it to anyone unless you're forced to."

Drummond handed each of them several pieces of paper. "These are your manumission papers, a bill of sale that says I bought you in Atlanta and a personal letter from me. Keep them in the pouch and around your neck all the time. You don't know when you might be made to show them." He handed each of them five dollars in change and currency to go in the pouch with the letters. "In case you need something for an emergency."

*

Early in the morning well before sunup, they climbed into Drummond's buggy. Sally was still disguised as a grieving young white woman. August took the reins and pulled away from the barn. Drummond seemed content to look out the window while the cool morning air surrounded him.

After a few minutes, he took Sally's hand. "I want you to know that when you get to the next station, you will be in the hands of another conductor and he will take good care of you. But I don't want you to think you are safe. It is still very dangerous up there. The slave hunters are everywhere and they can be extremely violent. Even if they can't prove you're escaped, they will steal you and sell you. As pretty as you are, they may just keep you for themselves."

"I understand uncle. August is a good man. He will protect me."

August pulled under the sign for the *Drummond & Mills Freight Co.* next to the river. *The Belle of Rochelle* was docked at the wharf. Tall black smokestacks were already pumping out thick smoke and sparks, much like the locomotives in Atlanta. After he tied the reins to the post and unloaded the trunks, Drummond left instructions for the manager and led the pair onto the boat.

Neither had ever been on a boat before. The *Belle* was a freight hauling, side-wheel riverboat that ran regularly from Chattanooga to New Orleans, moving freight in both directions. They also carried a few passengers when there was room. The *Belle* had six small cabins, including the captain's. Most of the space was dedicated to cotton, their most valuable customer.

"This is our first riverboat," said Drummond. "We have a second one on order from the Pringle Boat Building Company in Brownsville, Pennsylvania." The waiting ship was an earlier model of a Pringle built boat, one that had been in service for years. At nearly a hundred and eighty feet long with a twenty-nine-foot beam, it could hold over two-hundred tons of cotton and another twenty tons of miscellaneous freight.

Drummond always thought it was one of the most beautiful things he'd ever seen. Medium in size for a Mississippi River boat and painted white with red trim, the twenty-eight-foot-tall side wheels were impressive. The covers of the side wheels were painted with *Drummond & Mills Freight Co. Chattanooga, Tennessee.* The twin steam boilers required thirty cords of firewood a day. On top of the captain's bridge an oversized thirty-one-star American flag flew in the breeze. *All this and the whole craft draws less than three feet when full, a masterpiece of the boat builders' craft,* thought Drummond.

Sally and August were led into a small windowless interior cabin with a bed, table and two chairs. "Sally, you will sleep here and I will be right next door. August, come with me, I'll show you where you will sleep." Below the freight deck, just past the end of the boiler, was a narrow room with several pallets on the floor. Behind that was a smaller, separate space with a single pallet. Mounted on the wall was a heavy iron ring with ten-foot chain attached. On the end of the chain was a pair of leg shackles. "This is for you boy, stand still now." The boiler engineer watched as Drummond attached the shackles. Walking past the man, Drummond stopped. "If my nigger gives you a problem, you come and get me — understand?"

"Yessir Mister Drummond. I'll do it. Good to see you again."

There were no other passengers on this trip, but he trusted nobody, including the ten members of his crew. The reward for escaped slaves was just too tempting.

With a full load of cotton bales, pieces of machinery, and dozens of crates on board, the crew cast off the lines and merged slowly into the current of the Tennessee River. The boat would take several days before it connected to the Ohio River at the little town of Paducah Kentucky. There, the boat would take on wood and water but nothing else. The last run to Cairo would be short, reaching the wharf about sunup.

*

Cairo Illinois sits at the exact junction of the Ohio and Mississippi rivers. It had become a hub of the river freight industry in the area, only St. Louis was bigger. A dozen or more riverboats came and went from both rivers every day and the Illinois Central Railroad just completed the first direct route from Chicago to Cairo.

The railroad billed itself as having the first route all the way from Chicago to New Orleans. The rails ended in Cairo, but company-owned riverboats ran the rest of the route on the Mississippi. *The Belle of Rochelle* would take its cotton to a buyer in Baton Rouge, go down to New Orleans, and head back with a full load of dry goods on the return trip.

The weather had been good and the river smooth when they docked in Cairo. The side wheeler nosed up to the bank and lowered the gangway. Within minutes the boat was a scene of frenzied activity. Deckhands moved some of the crates from the boat to the docks and took on consignments of others. When finished, they filled all the empty space and tied down the load.

Drummond walked down the gangway arm and arm with his niece. She was dressed in a dark red dress, trimmed in black and a matching hat with a black veil pulled low over her face. Walking behind them was August, unkempt and dirty looking with his head down and his hat pulled low. He shuffled along slowly, the shackle chain between his ankles dragging behind. His wrists were shackled, but the chain normally connecting both had been removed.

One of the men moving crates watched them pass by. "Whatcha got there Mister Drummond? A runner?"

He nodded and poked August with his cane. "He thought he was, but he didn't make it. As soon as I get my niece home safe,

42

he's headed back to Macon and the leather. I doubt he'll try it again"

Walking up the bank to a waiting carriage, he helped Sally climb in and ordered August to sit in the back with the trunks. Drummond snapped one shackle to his wrist and one to the carriage. The driver cracked his whip and the horses lurched forward into the busy street. The docks were a blur of activity, freight wagons and people on foot and horseback crowded around the buggy.

Two men on horseback fell in behind the buggy. They both carried rifles on their horse and pistols at their waist. They watched August as the buggy maneuvered through the traffic.

"Boy — hey boy, " said the one closest to August. "I'm talking to you boy — answer me."

August didn't speak. He just kept his head down and looked away.

The stranger closed the distance to the buggy and stared hard at him. "You ain't a runaway nigger, are you boy? You look like a southern nigger, are you a southern nigger boy?"

Angus Drummond slowly rolled up the rear curtain to see who was talking. Sliding the business end of a double barrel shotgun out the opening, he cocked both hammers.

"Put your head down boy, I wouldn't want you to catch any of this buckshot when I shoot this no-good slave-huntin' son of a bitch."

"Hold on mister," said the rider. "I have the right to catch escaped slaves, I was just checkin' to see if this might be one."

Angus slid the shotgun farther out the window. "This boy is mine, and you got ten seconds to disappear from my sight before I load you up with buckshot." The riders quickly dropped back and disappeared into the crowd.

"Nothing I hate more than a filthy goddamn slave hunter," said Drummond as he put the shotgun back under the seat.

By mid-afternoon they came to a farm north of town and the driver circled the buggy to the back of the house. Handing the reins to a young boy, they all climbed down and walked to the house. Inside, they were greeted by a pleasant-looking middle aged woman with long brown hair and two children at her side. "Hello, I'm Marie. This is Will and Susan, the older boy outside is Isaac."

The carriage driver walked into the room and hung up his coat. "Angus, good to see you again, it's been a while. How are our newest passengers doing?"

"Good to see you too William. I think after a good meal and a night's sleep they'll be up for another journey."

"Uncle, are we in a free state now?" asked Sally.

"Sally, August," said Drummond, "you are now resting in the free state of Illinois."

The Free State

A large meal of ham, greens, and fresh bread, waited for them in the morning. With the curtains still closed, William led them into the sitting room. "I want to tell you about the next part of your journey. Angus will return to his home in Macon and I will be leading you from here."

"But are we not in a free state right now mas'r William," asked August, holding Sally's hand tightly. "Are we now free?"

"Yes, you are in the free state of Illinois. But because we are so close to other slave states like Missouri and Kentucky, it's much too dangerous for the two of you to go outside alone. The government made a terrible law that says slave hunters can go anywhere they want to look for runaways and nobody can stop them. That's why we need to get you farther away from here."

"What does farther away mean mas'r? How many more days of travel is that?"

"I will take you as far as the city of Chicago. It will take a long ride on the train to get there. The Chicago conductor will decide how to get you to Canada from there."

They had both heard of Canada but knew nothing about it until now. "Is Canada a free state uncle?"

"Canada is a different country. All of Canada is free, there are no slaves up there. Most who have escaped go to Canada and never come back."

"We are ready to go to Chicago, or to this country called Canada," said August. "Can we leave soon?"

"Soon enough. However, we have some preparations to make first. In the morning we will get everything ready. For now, just rest and have a good meal."

Sally and August were directed into a small darkened room behind an enormous hall tree. When they were in for the night, Marie pushed the furniture back against the wall. There was a pallet and blankets and a shelf with a jar of water and several biscuits. There they spent the time talking about their future and holding each other. He had never experienced anything like this before. He was warm, well-fed, and lying next to the most beautiful girl he'd ever seen. Stroking her hair, he touched her breasts and kissed her gently. She moved his hand down to her stomach. "Our child is growing, are you happy?"

"I am happy. More than you could imagine. We will have us our own family soon and a free country for him to live in."

*

Isaac waited with the two-horse carriage while William and Sally climbed into the back. Drummond hugged Sally and shook hands with August. "Good luck my friends. I know you will find a good life up north."

"Goodbye uncle. We will never forget what you have done for us," said Sally.

"Thank you mas'r," said August.

"Hopefully in a few days you will never need to call anyone mas'r again," said Drummond.

"August," said William, "everything is the same as it was with Angus. I am taking my niece home for her mother's burial. You are my slave that I will return to Macon after I get home. Oh also, my son Isaac will come with us. On the train he will be Sally's cousin who is accompanying her home. He's done this many times before and will be a great help."

It was a short ride to the Illinois Central Terminal from the house. Placing his carriage and horse with a local livery, they walked the distance to the new passenger building and sat down on a bench by the door. When the train came to a full stop, the conductor stepped off and looked around. When he saw William, he walked over and shook his hand. "What have you got for me today?"

"Just the one nigger is all. If you can keep him shackled 'til we get off in Chicago, it would be much appreciated," said William, handing him several coins.

"I will. He'll never get out of the mail car 'til you're ready for him, I assure you of that."

Sally had never been this close to something so large and scary before and stared at the giant, smoking beast for a minute. "Don't worry, this engine is the best one in the business. It's even fit up with carbide lighting inside and out for running at night. The headlamp can let the engineer see for half a mile and the seats are padded. That's good for a stove-up old man like me."

The three travelers boarded the second passenger car and found an empty seat in the rear. Sally went in first with Isaac next to her. William sat on the aisle. It was the best way to keep Sally away from the eyes of the other passengers.

The engine blew its whistle several times and lurched forward, causing everyone to grab hold of something for balance. As they began to pick up speed, the fine grit from the wood smoke filtered in through the windows and doors, causing more than one fit of coughing in the car. After a few minutes, the train reached speed and the smoke blew past the cars rather than into them.

After a long uneventful ride, and several stops for wood and water, the train rolled into the Chicago station through a maze of tracks and train cars and came to a stop at the passenger platform.

When the car cleared, William and Isaac helped Sally to the platform where she took a seat on the bench. While Isaac sat alongside holding her hand, William went back to the mail car and collected August. With his feet and hands shackled, he continued to walk with his head down slightly behind him. Sally checked that her veil was secure as they walked through the crowd of mostly white faces to a waiting cab. "Head west and I'll direct you from there," said William, handing the driver some money. The cab, a small stagecoach, was big enough for six inside. The leather trunk went into the rear boot and August rode on top shackled to the rail. William picked it in particular because they could pull down the curtains and not be seen.

After a day's ride they turned into a narrow farm road thickly lined with mature maples, oaks, and walnut trees. Across a small fast running creek was a farmhouse surrounded by freshly cleared forest on three sides. William paid the driver and watched as he disappeared through the trees. August stood nervously, waiting to see what was next.

Removing the shackles, William threw them into the barn. "If everything goes right, this is the last time you will ever have to feel the weight of captivity."

"Are we now free mas'r?"

William nodded, "August, you never need to call anyone mas'r again. You and Sally are officially free in the eyes of the law, but we do have many things to teach you yet. You must stay here on this farm for a while until you learn it all."

Sally broke down in uncontrollable sobs, embracing August and holding him tight. "Our child will be born free . . ." She continued to sob in great heaving bursts of tears.

He embraced her and held her until the sobs began to slow. "I love you and our child; we can now be a proper family."

"Sally, you can remove your hat and veil now if you'd like," said Isaac.

Almost before he could finish the sentence, the hat and veil sailed through the air and into the fresh dirt. She kissed August and she locked her arm in his. "We're ready Mister William, whatever you need us to do, we're ready."

*

The owners of the farm were an older couple named James and Emma. They showed the travelers into the house and offered them a meal. "William, how much do they know about the next step?" asked John.

"Not much, but they are willing to do whatever you say to make things work."

"Good enough. August, do you know anything about growing corn?"

"Never grew corn before, but I grew wheat and rice and did nearly everything there was to do on those farms, if that helps sir."

"Please call me James. Have you worked with horses and cattle before?"

"Yessir, I worked with pigs and sheep and goats too."

"Sally, what did you do where you were before?"

"I worked in the garden and I did cookin' too."

"I think this could work out quite well. Here is what I propose. I just bought this farm and cleared the land. We just finished burning all the stumps and I'm getting ready to put in my first crop of corn. However, breaking the ground for the first time is difficult work. There are enough rocks and roots still there that it will take a lot of sweat to get the plow through it, in time I will have more workers. That's what the other cabins are for, but right now it's just us. I can start you on the way to Canada in two days if that is what you want, but it is a very strenuous trip, especially for a woman with child. If you would agree to stay and work here for the first year while we establish this farm, we will take good care of you. Sally, you will have all the help you need when the baby comes and you and August will have a place of your own to live in as long as you're here."

"Would we be able to come and go as we please?"

James nodded. "That's what it means to be free. But I do insist that I teach you about the dangers of living around here first. Then you can come and go as you please, and I will also pay both of you."

They looked at each other and the answer was obvious. Tears ran down her cheeks and she buried her head in August's chest. "We would like very much to stay and work for you."

"Wonderful! Welcome to Sugar Grove Illinois and the Maple Leaf Farm. We will get you settled into your cabin today. Tomorrow we will walk the property and lay out the furrows for our very first crop. I have two of John Deere's brand-new *Improved Clippers*, the newest plow on the market, sitting in the barn ready to go. Even on tough virgin ground, with two of us plowing with two mules pulling we should do at least two acres a day. Sally, Emma likes to garden and it could be your job to assist her with it and in the kitchen as she needs. She will show you the cabin now."

They followed Emma to a small, freshly built cabin about a hundred yards behind the farmhouse. It was one of several that had been built from the recently cleared trees on the property. Emma pushed the door open and motioned for them to go inside. The room was about fifteen feet by twenty feet and the smell of fresh cut wood still remained. The north wall had a stone fireplace with a long mantle reaching from one side wall to the other. A hearth of smooth black stone spread out in front for three feet.

"How many will we be Missus Emma," asked Sally.

"What do you mean how many?"

"I mean how many will be living in here?"

The question took her a moment to understand. "There will only be the two of you, at least until the baby comes."

"All this cabin jus' for the two of us? There's room for many more if need be."

"Oh no, there's just enough room for you and August and the baby. You wouldn't want anyone else here, would you? You would never have any privacy."

There was a bed on one side of the fireplace with a thick pad and several blankets on it. "You may have to tighten the ropes on the bed as the fresh wood dries and there's more blankets if you need them," said Emma. "I had James put in extra shelves on the side of the fireplace and you have a skillet and two cooking pots. There is an endless supply of firewood out back and you will share a privy with the cabin next to you. A good spring is about fifty paces back in the trees, so water is no problem.

A long table, two benches, and two extra chairs were in front of the fireplace. August had been quietly playing the captured slave the whole trip from Macon and was finally beginning to relax. "I don't know what to say Missus Emma. We never had nuthin' like this before."

"Well you do now. For as long as you are here, this will be your home."

*

After a good breakfast and a second cup of tea, William and Isaac prepared to leave. "August, you and Sally will be well cared for. Come here and shake my hand like a free man does."

August shook his hand with a powerful grip and Sally hugged him. "Thank you for everything William. After all that you have done for us, I realize I don't know your last name."

"That's just the way it has to be. If you don't know my name then you can't reveal it to anyone else if you were ever caught. I hope you understand. Do you both have the paperwork Angus gave you?"

"Yessir, we do. We will never forget what you have done."

"Emma, I will take William and Isaac to the train station and be back in a while. It might be a good time to lay out your new garden and I will look for seed while I'm in town."

As they walked back to the house, Emma slid her arms into theirs. "Are you absolutely sure that this is what you want to do? Most want to go to Canada right away."

"We are for sure Missus Emma," said August. "We are not afraid of work and it's quiet here. But I have a question please."

"Certainly, what is it?"

"Can you teach us to read? We both want to learn to read the book about Jesus. On the farm they read to us from the book, but none of us could read it on our own."

"The book? You mean the Bible?"

"Don't actually know the name."

"I promise I will have you reading and writing before the corn is ready to pick," said Emma. "And we have many other things here that you can read. Do you know your numbers?"

He shook his head. "We don't know any numbers."

"Then we will start tomorrow."

"Start what tomorrow?" asked James as he walked into the cabin.

"They want to learn to read and write and do numbers. I told them I'd have them reading by the time we picked the corn."

"You are brave students," said James. "She can be a tough teacher."

"We are ready."

"Good, everything starts tomorrow. Be here when the sun comes up. For now, why don't you go fix up your cabin and be back at sunset for the evening meal?"

"Thank you. We will be back for supper."

"And August, our names are James and Emma Hanson. If you are to stay and work for me, you need to know that."

"Mister Hanson, we are August and Sally, but we never had no last names before . . ."

The Confederate

Leesburg, Virginia, October 21, 1862

The Battle of Ball's Bluff

He lay half-buried in a scattered stack of dead bodies at the bottom of the bluff. The grays and the blues were mixed together at the edge of the river and ice was already forming on the wet corpses. A few whiffs of frozen breath could be seen rising from the bloody pile. Several of the bodies had begun to wash down the river.

He stuffed his scarf against the wound on his hip with his right hand, slowing the bleeding slightly. His left hand held on to a tree root and his feet dangled in the river. The current had sucked the boots from his feet.

"Help me! Please, I need help!"

"Tucker? Is that you?"

"Yes, down here . . . please, I need help . . ."

"Hold on, we're coming." Three gray-coated men stepped over the dead soldiers all around him, grabbed him and pulled him through the mud. "We got you private."

He woke up on a table with a filthy sheet over him and two men in bloody white coats looking down at him. "Are you private George Washington Tucker of the Forty-Ninth?"

His head pounded and his vision was blurry. The stench of blood and death was overpowering and he was shaking from the cold. "I am, are you a doctor?"

"For the moment," said the man, making a note in his book. "You have a Yankee ball in your right hip close to your spine and I can't get it out without doing more damage. I've cleaned it the best I can and sewed you up. You're just going to have to try and live with it."

"Will I be able to walk?"

"Maybe in time with a cane, but you will always have difficulty."

Tucker lifted his head enough to see a row of tents and another soldier on a table with two doctors bent over him. Turning his head the other way, he saw a pile of arms and legs, some with boots and gloves still on. Behind the limbs were rows of dead soldiers covered by bloody sheets. He looked up at the doctor just as he injected him in the hip.

"Morphine, it will help with the pain. I'll give you more when this wears off. We don't have enough liquid but we have pills, enough that you can have some with you until you get home." The doctor finished wrapping his wound. "You guys really gave old General McClellan and his bluecoats what for out there. You took more than five-hundred prisoners and killed a bunch more. They're saying the river will take a bunch of them all the way to Washington, a good place for them if you ask me."

Two weeks later he was given a bottle of morphine pills, crutches, civilian clothes and a pair of used boots. He didn't want to think where they might have come from. He was discharged from the hospital, mustered out of the army, handed twenty-one dollars in confederate scrip and told to go home.

"Your war is over son," said the man behind the desk.

After several days of long, painful train rides and even rougher wagon rides, he made his way back to the family farm in Catawba County, North Carolina. Sitting in the cabin with his mother,

Polly, and brother, Levi, he drank a cup of tea and listened to Levi talk about the war.

"George, the Federals are on the run. All we have to do now is push 'em back up north and slam the borders shut on them. I plan on gettin' me a few Yankee hides before it's all over."

Shifting on the rocking chair, he pushed the padding down a little farther to help soften the pain. "Levi, please don't do it. Mother needs you here to run the farm. I'm no good for anything right now and I don't know if I ever will be."

"I'll wait until spring and help get the seed in, but then I'm gone. I don't want the war to end before I get there."

"Levi. You just don't understand . . ."

*

The telegraph office in Newton was always crowded with people waiting to hear news about the war. Leaning heavily on one crutch, George Tucker listened to the telegraph click off the latest information. Although still lean, or "skinny as a telegraph pole" as his mother liked to say, Tucker was now stooped over and bent to one side.

The operator always gave it to the recipient himself. He wanted to be certain the whole town didn't learn someone else's business. Looking around the room, he spotted Tucker standing by the door. His thick shock of curly red hair stood out in the crowd. Folding the message in half he walked over to him. "George, this is for you and your mother.

Tucker stepped outside and leaned against the building. The telegram read: *To Mrs. Polly Tucker: Private Levi T. Tucker - wounded in action, Wilderness, Virginia - 07-May 1864. Taken prisoner by Union forces, probable internment - Lynchburg, Virginia.*

The news was devastating to Tucker, and he knew it would be worse for their mother. She had been in failing health for months and this was sure to make it worse. When he got home, he sat down and put his arm around her. To his surprise she didn't cry.

She just squeezed his hand and looked at him. "Levi is in the hands of God. He'll make the decision to heal him or take him home." Two weeks after the telegram, she passed away in her sleep.

After burial next to their father, George had a polished white marble stone placed on their grave. It said: *R.I.P. Mary 'Polly' Knipe Tucker - 01-22-1800 / 07-20-1864. John Kenton Tucker - 10-16-1797 / 04-12- 1858. Mother and father of sons George and Levi, proud North Carolina soldiers.*

Standing on the porch, Tucker surveyed the farm and the slaves he had inherited. Growing cotton had been a tough proposition when his father bought this farm. He had cleared a hundred and sixty acres of trees and stumps by himself before any farming could be done. He also built a house, barn, cotton shed, three slave cabins, fenced off two pastures and dug a well before they even broke the ground for their first crop.

As small children, George and Levi Tucker grew up playing alongside the black kids while their fathers and mothers worked the fields. When the brothers got old enough to run the farm, the black workers they had played with were already spending ten or twelve hours a day in the fields. Like many planters, there was no field work on Sunday.

On a drizzly, cold day during harvest time, Levi heard shouting from the cotton shed. "Mas'r, mas'r! Hurry quick! Mas'r John is needin' help!" John Tucker lay face down on the ground between the gins in a pile of cotton hulls. After fifteen years of building the farm, his heart had given out. *Too much work for too many years*, thought Levi, as he gently brushed the cotton from his face.

George and Levi buried him in the family cemetery. The stone was a carved sandstone slab with 'R.I.P. John Tucker' on it. They would replace it with a nicer stone for him later.

By the start of the war, the brothers had acquired another hundred-and-sixty acres and added it to the farm. To handle the extra work, they invested in more slaves and built more cabins in the quarter. They were rapidly becoming one of the most prosperous farms in the county. As the brothers saw it, the system worked well. Just feed the blacks, give them a shack to live in, and a partner in their bed and they would work the cotton and make new babies for the farm.

Their father had never seen the need for an overseer. If there was punishment to be given, he handled it himself. For the first time, the Tucker Cotton Farm had three slaves escape. One strong buck, his wife, and their young son were missing. With the added workers, the brothers decided it might be time to look into hiring an overseer to keep the workers in line. They contracted a slave hunter, put up a reward for the escapees, and hired an overseer named Lucas Taggart.

"Mister Tucker, it's hard to keep them niggers from wantin' to try escapin' when they're this far north," said Taggart. "I think if you sell a couple south down to Charleston, that might help their attitude improve."

"Improving their attitude is why we hired you Mister Taggart," said George. "That escape cost us more than fifteen hundred dollars, plus two hundred for the slave hunters, and we never got them back. If you can't control them, we'll find someone that can. Understand?"

"I understand sir. I'll keep them minding the cotton, trust me."

*

Standing on the porch looking across the fields, George Tucker knew what he had to do. Another telegram in his hand informed him of the death of Levi while in the Lynchburg prison camp. With no wife and no family left but himself and the war still raging, he knew it was time to get out of the cotton business. If the North won the war, he would likely be out of business anyway, at least business as it had always been. "I don't see the South winning this war," he said to his neighbor over the fence one day.

"Tucker, I disagree wholeheartedly with that. But even if we do lose, someone has to grow the cotton."

"Sure, but with slavery gone, who will take care of the fields?"

"George, the niggers have nowhere to go. We just hire them as indentured servants and pay them a few coins. I'm not concerned, nobody would want them anyway. They ain't no good for nuthin' else."

"If you really feel that way, then why don't you buy my place? It would give you the biggest farm in the area and make you a very rich man."

After the sale of the farm, Tucker had a pocket full of cash but no plan. He remained in Catawba County for a while, living in a rented room in Newton, and buying a small livery business in town. On May 9th, 1865, the crowd burst out of the telegraph office with the news: "The war is lost — the South has surrendered!" yelled one man at the top of his lungs. The streets of Newton filled with people screaming and crying in disbelief.

Tucker leaned on his cane, watching from the front of the livery. He was seeing his prediction come true and was happy to be out of the cotton business. Now that the war was over, he would have to find a way to fit in, maybe even somewhere in the North. He no longer wanted to be part of the confusion that was about to take place in the South. The idea of having to do whatever the Northern politicians have in mind wouldn't set well with the Southern turn of mind. The idea of working alongside the blacks or worse, possibly even working for one of them was not going to sit well for him or any respectful southern businessman.

After several years of running the livery he met a Newton woman named Caroline Gassert, the daughter of a local dry goods store owner. Very tall and painfully thin with wildly thick, curly red hair and a face full of freckles. She was smitten with Tucker and made no secret of it. Walking into the dry goods store one afternoon, Tucker was immediately met by her at the counter.

"Mister Tucker, my name is Caroline Gassert and my family owns this store. I have heard that you have no family, is this true?"

Surprised by what he was hearing, he stared at her for a minute.

"I know who you are. It is true that I have no family, but what business is it of yours?"

"Forgive me for being so blunt, but I have a proposition for you."

"A proposition for me? Whatever are you talking about?"

"I think you are a handsome man Mister Tucker. Even with your bent and crooked body, I am attracted to you. I am just a gawky red-headed girl with no prospects for the future, so here's my proposition. I would like a family of my own, specifically a husband and children. I am smart and hard-working. I can do anything needed in any business you should choose."

"You want me to marry you? Is that what you're saying?"

"Yes, that's it exactly. Look at us, what other opportunities do you see for us here in Newton? We are two people who have no one. Why not be two people who have each other?"

"Miss Gassert, I have never heard anything quite like this before. Nor have I ever met any woman so forward as you. However, I do admit that your proposition is intriguing. Allow me time to give this some thought. I will see you here this time tomorrow with my answer."

Tucker couldn't believe what had just happened. This morning he was wondering what he would do with himself. The livery was making barely enough to pay the bills and he'd already decided to sell it and move on. Now this woman had just changed everything with her crazy idea.

Tucker walked into the store the next morning. "Miss Gassert, if you and I are to be married, then you must call me George and I will call you Caroline. I would like three children, providing at least one of them is a son. If not, then we shall have a fourth. I shall take the best care of you and the children possible. You should know that I had planned on moving to St. Louis. The people of Missouri still have the sensibilities of good southern stock. I have a cousin there and he will help us get established."

"George, I would like to live with you in St. Louis. I think it could be a place with a lot of opportunity and a good place to raise our children."

Caroline Gassert became Mrs. George Washington Tucker the following Saturday. Her father provided a dowry of two hundred and fifty dollars and gave George a used revolver from his store, advising him to, "keep a sharp eye out things can get pretty wild out there."

Her mother and sister helped her put together a hope chest at the last minute, something she thought she might never need. The wedding was in the Gassert home and the local Methodist minister married them. Her mother and sister gave her a beautiful carved pink cameo broch attached to a fine lace collar as a wedding gift. Her mother pressed a small coin purse into her hand. "A woman needs a little money for herself, don't tell your father." After a few tears and hugs, the couple made their way to a waiting carriage.

The couple took a room at the best hotel in Newton and settled in for the night. Neither of them had ever been with a partner before. George was more nervous in that room than he had been facing the Yankee's at Ball's Bluff. After cleaning up for the evening, he walked back to the room, not exactly sure what to do next.

Caroline was already in the bed and under the blanket, her clothes folded neatly over the side chair. George sat on the edge of the bed without speaking, his back to his new wife. "George, will you come to bed now?"

He set his hat and cane on the table and started to remove his shoes. "Caroline, I've never been with a woman before."

"George, it's my first time also. If you would like I can close my eyes while you get undressed and under the blanket."

"I think that would be good please." After he undressed he quickly slipped under the covers.

Caroline put her arm around him and gently pulled him close. Laying together in each other's arms, the warmth of their bodies flooded over them. After a few minutes Caroline pulled off the blanket and they saw each other's body for the first time. Looking at him for several minutes, her fingers moved over the scar where the union ball rested against his hip. He touched her breasts and explored her body, running his fingers over her fair skin. Freckles covered her entire body, just like they did his. "I want to kiss you please."

"You don't have to ask, you're my husband. You may kiss me or touch me wherever you like, and I will do the same with you."

After they made love for the first time, they lay together wrapped in each other's arms. "George, did you ever think about our kids?"

"What about them?"

"With us as parents, they will undoubtedly have the reddest hair in St. Louis. Everyone will know the Tucker kids."

He laughed out loud. "Just like when I was a kid, everyone knew me because of my hair."

"I love you George . . ."

Selling the livery for a modest profit, he bought stage tickets to Nashville and they headed north. From there they would book river passage to St. Louis and a new life.

*

Waiting on the wharf for their luggage, the first thing that they noticed about St. Louis was the odor.

"George, I don't like this place already, I believe I might be sick."

"As soon as Theo gets here, we can get out of it," said Tucker.

George's cousin Theo pulled up in a one-horse carriage, jumped out and embraced his cousin. "And this must be your beautiful bride you wrote me about?"

"This is my wife Caroline," said Tucker. "Theo, can we go somewhere to get out of this rancid smell? It's about to make my wife ill."

"Let's get the luggage loaded and we can head home. You will stay with us for a while I hope?"

"Thank you for the offer, we would love the visit. Then we can sit down and talk about what opportunities may be found in St. Louis for this old soldier."

The ride took about an hour. The newlyweds were amazed at how large the city was. It was said to be the fourth largest in the country. Never had they seen so many smoke stacks and experienced such a variety of smells. "Theo, does it always smell this bad?

"Well, it's worse than usual today, but when the wind blows it's much better."

Pulling up in front of a substantial red brick house, he tied up the horse and invited them in. His wife and two daughters greeted them and showed Caroline to their room. "Theo, what exactly is your business? You said in your letter you made paint?"

Theo nodded. "I own a factory that makes all different kinds of paint. In particular we make paint for barges and things like rail cars and river boats. The boat that brought you here was likely carrying our paint."

The next morning the men sat on the porch looking at the city. "Theo, I notice that the air is much clearer here, even though I can see it hanging over the city."

"We're west of town on higher ground and we get the first of the breezes from the northwest. It's one thing to work down there; you need to make a living. But I don't know why anyone would live down there, some days the smells are unbearable. What is it that you want to do now that you're here? I can give you work at the paint factory if you think that's something you want."

"I appreciate the offer, but I have some money that I may want to invest, or maybe get a small business of my own."

"Tomorrow we will go to town and I will introduce you to some of my friends. They may have a few suggestions for a new St. Louis citizen."

*

The big room in the St. Louis Businessman's Club was ornate to the point of being obnoxious. Dozens of tables were covered in white cloth and set with fine china and silver. It was the kind of place that George had only heard about in the past.

A black man with short gray hair and a proper fitting suit escorted them to a back table where four men were already seated.

The waiter took their order. "George, what would you like to drink?"

"Uh, maybe a whisky?"

"Anything you want George, I'm buying."

"Whisky's fine, thank you."

After the drinks came and they had placed their lunch orders, Theo made the introductions all around. A man named Cecil spoke first. "So George, Theo says you fought for the South?"

"Yessir. Still carry a Yankee ball in my hip from the Battle of Ball's Bluff at Leesburg."

"Damn George, I heard that you really shot the hell outta old McLellan and his pack of Yankee dogs, that true?"

"It is. We ran them back into the Potomac River and let their bodies float all the way down to Washington."

"Well you're in good company here, we're proud to know you. We're all southern men ourselves and we should all stick together. Near the end of the war, we could see that the south was losing, so we sold everything and took our money to Missouri. The people here still think like we do. I still couldn't stand the thought of moving to a northern state like Illinois. We've all done quite well since we got here."

"That's why I'm here now. I could see no place for me in North Carolina after the surrender, so I sold my cotton business about six months before it ended, got married, and headed north. What kinds of things did you invest in?"

"All kinds of things. Theo's in the paint business, we're in brewing, rendering, lumber, and I'm in brick making."

"What would you advise for a newcomer?"

"If it were me," said Cecil, "and I had some money to invest, I'd consider getting into whisky distilling."

"I think that's good advice cousin," said Theo. "A lot of people are getting rich in that business. I know of a couple of places that are looking for investors right now. It appears they can't make the stuff fast enough. While we are looking at opportunities for you, maybe Caroline would be interested in working in our office, I could use a new bookkeeper."

"Would she be working in the factory?"

"No, she would be in the office, she wouldn't have to go into the factory for anything."

"I'll ask her tonight. When can we see the whisky operations?"

"I'll set it up for tomorrow."

*

Both distilleries were near the river on the east edge of town, just below the beautiful new Eads Bridge over the Mississippi River. "This is a great location George. We no longer have to depend on the ferries or the riverboats to move our products east. The bridge has a railroad and a freight road into Illinois. The riverboat business is dying; more trains and roads will soon put them out of business. We can now load our wagons here and cross into Illinois and points east."

The first distillery they looked at was a two-story frame building, set back from the river about a quarter mile. Walking through the mud into the building, the smell of bourbon in the building was powerful. "Occupational hazard," said Theo. "Though I could get used to it."

"This place is filthy Theo. Look at the floors. It doesn't look like they ever clean up the mud. I can see a hole in the roof from here and birds in the rafters."

"Do you want to meet the owner?"

"No, I want to leave. I want no part of this."

The next business was a solid brick building, only about two hundred yards from the river. It was surrounded by good packed gravel and had a separate barn for their horses and wagons. The owner met them at the door. "You must be George Tucker? Good to meet you, I'm Alexander Hope, this is my operation." Tucker shook his hand and followed him into the building.

The odor of bourbon was just as strong, but the operation looked clean and neat. The largest room was filled with rows and rows of oak barrels filled with whisky. A dozen men were working on the distillery floor and several teams of draft horses waited for their wagons to be loaded. "Mister Hope, do you handle all the shipping yourself?"

"We do everything within fifty miles of St. Louis from here. If it's farther away, we contract it out. Theo and Cecil both say you're a good southern man and you're looking to invest in a business in the city."

"I am, but I don't really know anything about the distilling business."

"You don't really need to worry much about the distilling process, just about the finances. We know it's a good product because we sell it as fast as we can make it."

"If you're doing so well, why do you need another investor?"

"We need to expand. I bought the ground to the west of us, but I have no money left for the new storage and shipping building. Once we get it up, I can enlarge the distillery floor."

"Alexander, let me talk with my wife tonight and I will be back tomorrow with my answer."

"I will see you tomorrow then."

George lay in bed next to Caroline. "I want to tell you about the investment opportunity I looked at today. It's a whisky distillery. They are a very good-looking operation and they need to expand to keep up with sales."

"Well, you know I don't get involved in your financial business. If you think this is the right thing, then you should do it."

"I believe I will go and talk to the owner tomorrow and see what the terms are."

"George, there's something I want to tell you . . . ."

"About the distillery?"

"No, about the baby."

"What baby?"

"Our baby . . ."

*

Riley Tucker was born with the wildest head of red hair anyone had ever seen on a newborn, just as Caroline had predicted. She had been working as a bookkeeper in the paint factory until she delivered him. After arranging for someone to care for him, she prepared to return to work. "George, I don't care what Theo says. That factory stinks, even in the office."

"Do you want to quit working there?"

"No, not right now. But as soon as we can find our own house I would like to stay home with Riley."

"Then we should start looking right away."

"The sooner the better. That place gives me headaches and makes me feel sick."

*

Tucker spent most of his days at the distillery, watching the new construction and learning the business. "Alexander, I don't understand some of the expenses in this ledger. Every month there's several hundred dollars going away and it doesn't say where. Will you explain them to me please?"

"George, it's just the cost of doing business around here."

"What do you mean?"

Alexander shrugged. "You have to pay out a little to get the whisky into the best places, that's just the way it is."

"You mean bribes?"

"Call it whatever you want, everyone does it. Like I said, it's just the cost of doing business."

*

George took Caroline on a carriage ride the following Saturday, looking at available homes for sale on the Northwest edge of St Louis. After finding one that they both agreed on, they made an offer. "It would not be available for a while," said the seller's agent. "The owner just passed away and the family is feuding over the money from the sale. The attorney assures me that it will be no more than six months, eight at the most."

"George, I want this house. If I have to wait for it I will."

"You're sure? We can look at the others if you would like."

"No. I'll keep working at Theo's stinky factory until then. We can use the extra money for new furnishings."

With the house finally ready to move into, George began to gather up their possessions and take them to the new address. On the ride back to Theo's house, George confided in her that something at work was bothering him. "Caroline, I found out that Alexander pays out bribes to get his product in the best places. I don't think I can do business with him any longer."

"I understand George, but you should know something first."

"What's that?"

"There's another redhead on the way . . ."

The River Man

The celebration lasted long into the night. The citizens were justifiably proud of their small town's twenty-fifth anniversary. It had been a loud rowdy event, only disturbed by a few drunken fights between the working men firing pistols. The zinc miners and the coal miners challenged each other and they both called out the river men, telling them what they thought of their "easy" work on the steamboats and the canal boats.

The Illinois and Michigan Canal, a man-made waterway, connected Lake Michigan to the Mississippi River by way of the Illinois River, effectively creating a commercial waterway from the Great Lakes to the Gulf of Mexico. The little river town of La Salle had become a major player in the shipping business.

The canal boats traveled the ninety-six miles from Chicago to La Salle and back with passengers and goods of all kinds. In La Salle travelers could transfer to boats for the ride south or to Chicago. Local zinc, coal, and produce in season were shipped to anyone that wanted it. The future of the city looked good and more people were moving in every day.

Ezekiel Hobbs was already an old man on that anniversary day. Just how old no one knew for sure. Some of the locals had known him a long time and never heard him say more than a few words. When he did speak, he would often wave his Bible and launch into a long loud tirade about all the sinners in town. They knew he lived with a woman thought to be his third or fourth wife. They also knew he had three beautiful daughters of varying ages from about twenty-five, down to thirteen. All had long dark hair and fair skin and were considered quite attractive.

A son from some previous relationship used to live with them but was currently incarcerated in the state penitentiary for attempted murder of a dock worker. Another son had been shot and killed two years before by a coal miner over a woman.

The family lived on a sprawling, run-down farm east of town and made most of their living raising horses. Hobbs was one of the early river men on the canal and had provided mules for the canal boats until they switched over to steam power.

With his livelihood taken away by progress, he began to raise saddle horses and draft horses. Within a few years, he was well-known for his fine matched pairs of Percheron draft horses. He also kept two old mules' around to remind him of the old days. A few inches over five feet tall, he was built like a rain barrel with short muscular legs and powerful arms. His enormous hands and wrists looked out of proportion to the rest of his body and his left leg drug slightly from an old horse injury.

Locals liked to tell the story of a traveler who shook his hand to thank him for something and ended up with several broken fingers. The same locals also told stories about his ugly temper and that he had killed at least two men somewhere along the canal in the early days. They may have been just stories, but most men knew instinctively he was someone not to be trifled with. Generally though, he kept to himself, working his horses while the girls looked after the farm.

All three girls were experts at breaking and training horses and with guns. The oldest, Clara, and her sister Grayce, were regulars in town. Often seen selling or trading horses, they also bought all the supplies for the farm and on occasion stopped at one of the riverfront saloons for a whisky or two before heading home. Their mother didn't allow drinking in the house, so they stopped in town or snuck a pull from the bottle Ezekiel kept hid in the barn. The youngest daughter, Gemma, was only thirteen but was already an excellent rider and trainer.

Clara worked hard every day except Sunday. On Saturday she would work with the new colts or helped with the Percherons. After dark she headed for the LaSalle House, the town's biggest watering hole. Before the evening was over, she drank all the cheap whisky she could hold, started at least one fight, and found a partner for the night.

Sunday morning her mother would splash cold water in her face and tell her to get up and get her Bible. For the rest of the day, she was more miserable from reading the Bible and singing hymns, than she was from the previous night's whisky.

Ezekiel carried the good book with him wherever he went, and answered only to "Father" with his family, as though he were a self-ordained minister. In public he liked to present a picture of a pious believer, but the family knew better. Stiff and unbending, he saw the world only in his terms. He preached to his family about God and forgiveness, then physically punished them for the smallest infraction. He used a razor strop on his children and his hand on his wife. He would often fly into a drunken rage and beat his own horses, killing more than one prized animal over the years. The older he got, the greater the rage built inside him.

Sunday mornings were the worst time for the family. After his sermon, he would call out each family member for the week's transgressions, real or imagined. "Miss Clara Bea Hobbs, when will you ever learn? No good can come from all this dancing with the devil the way you do," said Ezekiel. "You will find a good Christian man and settle down before you get so old no one but Satan will want you."

"Well Father, a fine example you are. You're not exactly a perfect Christian man now, are you?"

Ezekiel's right arm flashed out in an instant and his fist caught her square on the jaw. She fell back onto the hearth spitting blood.

"You sorry old bastard. One day you will pay for that, I promise you. If anyone really knew the things you've done, they'd hang you from the nearest tree without a trial."

Ezekiel stepped forward and reached out, failing to get a hold on her. She jumped to the side and stood up. "Go find someone else to beat on old man. You're done here. Touch me again and I'll kill you . . ."

"You whore of Satan.! Get out of my house and don't ever come back!"

"I'm leaving, but hear me old man. I'm taking my possessions and a horse. You do anything to try and stop me and I'll have more than a few things to tell the sheriff."

Red in the face with spittle spewing from his mouth and shaking with uncontrollable rage, Ezekiel pointed to the door and screamed at her. "Get out now — you goddamn whore!"

Gathering up her meager collection of possessions, she went outside and saddled up her favorite horse, a beautiful, dappled, gray stallion, the finest horse the farm had ever produced. Ezekiel had turned down many offers for *River Man*, as he had named him the day he was foaled. The horse was a sixteen-hand package of power and speed. Clara had broken him and trained him and was the only person who ever rode him. *The old bastard couldn't even have gotten up on him, let alone ride him*, thought Clara.

She also chose a young mare that she liked and put a pack saddle on her, loaded her belongings, and headed down the lane. Turning onto the road, she went about a mile before Grayce caught up with her. "Clara, please — stop!" she said, finally catching her breath. "You can't leave us with him. You know what it will be like for us when he finds you're gone."

"Grayce, I don't want to leave, but I can't be around him anymore."

"Clara, he's been hurting us for a while now, just like he did you. I tried to keep him away, but he's too strong. If you're gone then I can't stay either. I'm afraid he's going to kill us or mother."

Clara got off the horse and held her sister. They sat down on the roadside and talked for a while. "Grayce, could you and Gemma and mother run the farm if he were gone?"

"We can. But wouldn't you be here if he was gone?"

"No. I'm moving on, I'll never come back here again. Maybe it's time to fix the problem once and for all. Okay. You go back to the farm and act like nothing is going on. Tomorrow night I'll come and tap on your window. When I do, you need to get father up and go outside. Tell him you think you heard a horse thief. Tell him you think maybe they are up at the old corral."

"Then what?"

"Just get him there and you'll see."

*

Several hours after sunset, Clara walked slowly through the woods to the cabin and tapped quietly on the window. Grayce opened it a few inches. "Give me five minutes and then wake father and tell him you think there is a horse thief out by the back corral."

70

Grayce got dressed and when the time had passed, she ran to her father's room, shouting, "Horse thief! Father, we have a horse thief!"

The old man pulled on his boots and grabbed his shotgun.

"Where did you see him?"

"I think he went out toward the old corral."

It had been overcast all day and started to rain lightly. Stumbling through the trees with his night shirt flapping, he reached the corral. He stood at the edge of the trees, shotgun up, trying to pick out the shape of a person in the dark.

Clara stepped from the trees and walked up behind him.

"Hello Father, . . ."

As the old man turned to look at her, she swung the axe with everything she had, hitting him in the left temple. Grayce walked up next to her. "My god Clara, you've taken off his head!"

"Well most of it anyway," said Clara, watching the blood drain into the mud. Leading River Man from the trees, she tied a rope from his saddle to the old man's feet. Grayce stood in stunned disbelief, unable to move or even cry. "Come on sister, we have to finish this."

They dragged him deep into the trees and stopped alongside a deep grave that she had dug earlier. The shower had turned into a driving rain, soaking everything. Rolling him into the hole, she threw in the axe and the shotgun and stripped off her clothes and threw them on the body. "Hurry up Grayce, strip now! You don't want anyone to find any blood, do you?"

As the two girls stood naked in the rain, they hugged for a moment then started to fill in the grave. Grayce's tears began to come in great heaving sobs. "It's all right Grayce, he won't ever hurt anyone again, it's all over," said Clara, hugging her tightly.

They worked silently for half an hour. When they were done, they covered the spot with leaves and small branches. The rain had washed away any blood on the ground or on the girls. "We have a family secret now Grayce, and we must take it to the grave with us. Do you understand?"

"I understand."

"Goodbye sister," said Clara, giving her a hug. "Get back home and dry off and go back to bed. When I find a place, I will send a letter."

Maple Leaf Farm

August looked down the furrows of the freshly plowed field. They were straight as a tight string, neatly following the gentle rise of the field, just the way he liked them. Leading the horse into the barn, he heard the hooves of a horse and creak of a wagon. "Hello over there," said a strange voice.

He turned to see a man driving a one-horse buggy and a skinny redheaded boy sitting next to him. "Stranger, what can I do for you?"

"My name is George Tucker, and this is my son Riley. I was told in town that this farm may have some work available. We are fresh from St. Louis and looking for work away from the big city."

"You don't have a woman?" asked August.

"My wife Caroline died in childbirth along with our second child, a daughter. She got sick and had trouble breathing. She was very weak when it was time to deliver. It's just me and Riley now," said Tucker. "Is the manager around?"

"I am the manager."

Tucker stepped down and leaned against the buggy wheel sizing up the man in front of him. "How is it a nigger such as yourself comes to manage such a fine farm as this?"

August remained rigid, staring at the stranger. "How is it that a pitiful, broke down Reb bastard like yourself dares to come so far

72

North? I'd guess that sorry-looking body of yours likely come from a Yankee rifle?"

Tucker nodded. "Still carry a ball from the Battle of Ball's Bluff and proud to have been there."

"Mister, I'm gonna tell you this just once. If you want to get along up here, you need to leave all that Reb crap at home, this ain't Missouri."

"How about the owner, is he around?"

"I am the owner."

"No disrespect meant. There just ain't no way a man can forget all that stuff."

"You ain't listenin' Reb. We all got things behind us we would like to forget about. If you want to get along up here you gotta get over it."

"Does that mean that you might have some work for me?"

"Maybe. If you and the boy can work good, then I got two things that need attention, animals and trees. You know much about them?"

"I worked horses and cattle all my life, even owned a livery once. Not sure what you mean about the trees though."

"We are corn planters, but we make some maple sugar every year for extra money. I can teach you, it's easy. Even a pitiful looking old Reb like you can do it. We also raise horses. We have a trainer and she has made us some great horses."

"She? You have a woman working your stock? Never seen that before."

"It's something else you'd have to get used to. If you work here, she'll be your boss."

"Is she like you?"

"Like me?"

"You know, a . . . a . . . negro?"

"Don't matter what color she is. One more thing Reb."

"What's that?"

73

"I ever hear you use the word nigger again — I will kill you."

Tucker shifted uncomfortably and stared at August. "Well then, what do I call you?"

"My name is August Freedman. My wife is Sally and my son is Jacob. His wife is Rose and my granddaughter is Hattie Rose. Clara Hobbs is in charge of all the horses. You suppose you can remember all that Reb?"

"So if I hire on here, you planning on calling me a Reb forever?"

"You want the job or not? I said I could use the help. Six days a week, one dollar a day plus a cabin and keep."

"I'll take it."

August reached out his hand and looked directly into his eyes.

Tucker realized he had never shaken a black man's hand before and hesitated for a moment.

"If you can't shake my hand then get the hell off of my land."

His enormous hand swallowed up Tucker's with a crushing grip causing him to wince at the pain. "You can turn your horse out into the lower pasture if you want. There's room in the barn for the buggy. Take the empty cabin out back, settle in there tonight. Work starts at sunup."

The next morning he introduced the new arrivals to Clara and Jacob. At seventeen years old, Jacob Freedman was tall, powerfully built, and very quiet. He had been born on the farm soon after August and Sally arrived, the first freeborn child of two escaped slaves. A sister named Alberta followed a year later.

By the time he was eight he could do almost anything on the farm. He loved to grow things and took care of all the planting and kept the best garden in the county. He didn't care much about horses but could harness one and plow from sunup to sundown. His cabin was the one farthest from the house, backed up against the maple trees. His wife Rose, was a pretty light-skinned girl about the same age. She did the cooking, helped with the garden, and cared for their daughter Hattie Rose.

After leaving the family, Clara Hobbs wandered a while, looking for something she wanted to do. Riding through Sugar Grove, she met James Hanson at the livery and they struck up a conversation about horses. He told her how much he admired *River Man* and invited her to come by the ranch for supper. By the end of the evening she had agreed to start raising horses for the farm. Her cabin sat between the barn and the place now taken by the Tuckers. She was never far from her horses.

When Tucker went to work on the farm, Clara had twenty horses that she had raised from colts, all out of *River Man,* the stallion she rode in on. By carefully choosing two good-looking mares from a breeder in Wisconsin, she built up a well-respected remuda that had a list of customers waiting to buy. She sold many of the mares and geldings, always holding back *River Man* and several good stallions and mares for the farm. She also supplied work horses and saddle horses for many of the farms in the area. The Hanson's paid for her work, and split the profits from the sale of horses with them.

Clara had left her wilder days behind her, choosing to stay close to the ranch unless she had horse business elsewhere. After six months she wrote a letter to Grayce, asking if anyone was looking for her. Several weeks later, she got a letter back.

Clara,
"Only two people came looking for father and it was about horses. After about a month, the sheriff came by and asked where he was and I told him he passed about two weeks ago and that we buried him out back. We had put up a marker we made out of barn wood and killed that mean old sow father kept. She is now moldering in the grave. The smell from the sow convinced the sheriff well enough. Mother knows what happened but does not speak about it. Come home for a visit someday.
Your sister, Grayce.

*

After she read the letter, she threw it in the fire and returned to the barn. George Tucker would assist her with the care of the horses. He had groomed and cared for horses since he was a kid. The one problem he hadn't mentioned was about the farrier work. Shoeing horses required grabbing a leg, pulling it up, and putting it over his knee or between his thighs while he worked on it. It meant bending over at the waist for long periods of time. He had done it a thousand times before, but now, after a few minutes of this, the Yankee ball began to rub and grind. In minutes the pain was unbearable.

To his relief, she told him that he didn't have to do the shoeing. "You won't need to work on their feet, I take care of that myself. Your job will be to keep them watered, fed, and clean. The stalls need to be cleaned every single day and the tack needs to be cleaned and hung up as well. Make sure that we have enough smith supplies. I want things kept clean at all times — you understand?"

"I do. I've done all this before."

"Make sure there's at least a week's worth of clean dry feed and fresh water inside the barn. Also, check with August. He's got a couple of steers he's fattening up. He might want you to take care of those, and a few hogs."

Tucker really wanted to tell her that he once owned a large farm and had a livery business, and that he wasn't about to take orders from a woman. He wanted to scream it to the heavens, but he understood that his place in this new world would depend on him holding his tongue. After losing his wife and baby in childbirth and his money in a bad business venture in St. Louis, he had nothing left but a buggy, one tired horse, an old colt pistol and his son, Riley.

"What brings you to this place," asked Clara.

"I was just looking for a new start for Riley and me. My wife Caroline got sick when she was pregnant and died in childbirth.

Our second child, a girl, was also lost." Tucker became emotional talking about it. The tears started to flow and he couldn't speak for several minutes. "I'm sorry, I haven't been emotional about anything until now."

"It's okay Mister Tucker, everyone here has had a lot of tragedy, we all understand. That's when you decided to move?"

"Please call me George. Shortly after that I lost all of my money in the distillery business. My partner was a crook. He went to jail for being part of something they're calling the whisky ring scandal. The government took our business away, so here we are, starting all over again."

"Well, this is a good place to start over. You will be glad to raise your son here."

"Clara, August said if I ever used a certain word again, he would kill me. Did he really mean that?"

"Yes."

Tucker leaned against the gate and thought about her answer, he decided to change the subject. "He also said something about maple sugar, do you know about that?"

"The sugar season's over. They tap the trees in the winter and get the sap in March and April. I don't have anything to do with that, I just work with the horses."

On Sundays, August and Sally had supper for everyone, followed by a short sermon and a discussion afterwards. Nobody on the farm had to attend, but it was a tradition that everyone had come to love. James Hanson had died a few years ago and Emma passed less than a year later. With no children of their own, and no one else to inherit the farm, they willed it to August upon their death. The idea of the Sunday meal and sermon had started with them. August and Sally loved the idea of everyone coming together to talk about the good book and continued the tradition.

George and Riley joined Clara and the family for supper. They had beef, ham, potatoes, and greens. Rose made bread and cornbread and August read from the Bible while Hattie Rose sat on his lap. The weather was cool enough to need a fire and they all settled in front of the fireplace. Sally offered tea to those who wanted it, a drink they learned to love from Emma Hanson. Tonight, August opened the Bible and began to speak. *"Ephesians 6:5 says: Servants, be obedient to them that are your masters according to the flesh, with fear and trembling, in singleness of your heart, as unto Christ."* Tucker wondered why he chose exactly that verse for his first supper.

*

Riley Tucker loved life on the farm. By the time he was fifteen, his curly red hair was famous all over the county. At seventeen he married Mary Daggart, a farm girl from Creston, a small-town west of Sugar Grove and they took a cabin for themselves. Within a year she delivered a boy they named Clancy Tucker. His red hair was even wilder and more prominent than his father's. By the time he was old enough for school, he was well known for fighting with anyone and everyone that teased him about his hair.

School work was always a challenge for him and he had never been scared of anything, except for spelling and numbers. He fought any attempt to get him to read, write, or do arithmetic. Eventually, the family gave up on the idea of keeping him in school. "As long as he works hard," reasoned Riley, "he'll get along fine."

When he was old enough, Clancy took over the job of gathering maple sap for the sugar from his father. Drilling a hole in the tree, inserting the spile and gathering the buckets of sap was fun for him. The long days alone in the forest and the sugar house were his private world. After he finished collecting the sap, he poured the clear liquid into a large pot and set it on the stove. The process of boiling down several hundred gallons of sap was long and tedious and required constant attention, but it suited his personality. He learned to carve molds in pieces of scrap wood to make the candy into the shape of hearts and crosses and other characters like butterflies. He would press the moist sugar into the molds and give the little pieces to the children. He loved to work, particularly hard physical work, and never seemed to find enough time to get it all done.

Hattie Rose, the daughter of Jacob and Rose Freeman (the "d" had been dropped from their name to make it easier to pronounce), had been Clancy's best friend since childhood. Much younger than her, he was already taller and heavier than her or anyone else his age. He watched out for her and walked with her whenever she left the farm. They made an odd couple, a pretty, petite black girl and an enormous, redheaded white boy with a barrel chest and arms like logs. One Sunday, after the sermon, she sat down next to Clancy, squeezed his hand, and announced their intentions to be married. They were married in the fall of the same year.

Clancy had always been the restless type; the farm work was okay but he wanted to see more of the country. He had always wanted to see the western mountains. Hattie had read many books to him and the ones that interested him were about the mountains and the settling of the West. He loved looking at pictures of the mountains and deserts, and of real cowboys. After a long talk with Hattie, he decided it was time to move west and see it for himself.

Maple Leaf Farm had three wagons used for general hauling. One of them, an ancient Studebaker high wheel model sat behind the barn covered in weeds and old lumber. Pulling it into the barn, Clancy realized he was looking at his way to the West. Originally an old grain hauler, the wagon was still sound and solid. Fitted with two and a-half inch steel tires, the hubs and wheels were all sound.

He replaced a few of the side boards and rebuilt the seat. Inside he built compartments and boxes to hold their possessions, and shelves on the outside to hold extra feed for the horses. After making a large sleeping pallet for them, Hattie fashioned a canvas top to keep out the weather. Repairing the necessary harness for the two-horse team, he felt as though they were ready for their adventure to the mountains.

"Where do you have in mind to go?" asked Riley.

"To see the Rocky Mountains of Colorado."

The farm had been their family's life and they had watched several generations grow up working the cornfields and the maple trees. Most of the old ones were buried on the same ground. The farm had started out in the middle of a wild undeveloped forest, and now was just one of many farms strung across the countryside.

Before leaving, Clancy and Hattie Rose walked back to the small family cemetery under the maple trees one last time and looked at the names on the stones. James and Emma Hanson, immigrants from Norway and early Illinois homesteaders, were laid together under a plain white marble stone. August and Sally Freeman, escaped slaves from a North Carolina rice plantation, lay next to them. Alberta Freeman, daughter, who died at age nine, lay next to Sally, under a smaller white stone. George Washington Tucker, former slave-owner and proud Confederate soldier wounded at Ball's Bluff, lay next to August with a simple gray marble marker.

The wagon was loaded and ready to go. Clara, now very thin and white haired, hitched two of her best mares to it and tied a young stallion on the back. "These will give you a good start on your own remuda," said Clara. Hattie hugged her. After saying the last of their goodbyes, Clancy hugged his father with tears in his eyes. "Father, Hattie and I feel we have to see more of the world and find our own place. I hope you understand that we love you."

"I understand. Your mother and father and my mother and father were all looking for a better life. It's just our nature to wonder what else there is out there."

The Mexican

At fifteen years old, Hector Garza stood just over five-foot four-inches tall. His dark skin and lean features displayed a mix of his Spanish and Guachilies Indian history. Considered quite handsome by the girls in town, Garza was often teased by his fellow workers about how many señoritas he could have if he wanted. Garza knew he wasn't ready for a girlfriend yet, not here in Zacatecas and not while he worked in the silver mine. Heck, as he had been called since he was a child, was a small man with a big plan.

The newly established Mexican Central Railway had arrived in Zacatecas a few months before and the excitement was still obvious from the crowds of people watching the black, smoking engine as it took on a fresh water supply. It was being readied for the trip to El Paso Del Norte. "I will be on the next train," he said out loud to no one in particular. "I will be on the next train to the United States of America very soon."

Walking back to his room, he thought of what he had heard about El Paso City from the traqueros, a rough group of older men living in shacks along the side of the rails. They traveled everywhere the trains ran and repaired the tracks. They had been to El Paso City many times.

"Very dangerous to those that are unprepared," said one. "You must carry a pistol for protection," said another.

He sat down on the side of his pallet. As he collected his thoughts, he reached deep into the straw and pulled out his small collection of possessions from a scrap of brown cloth. Opening it slowly, he removed the knife he found in the mine. He had repaired the handle with rawhide and made a sheath that could be worn on a belt.

Along with the knife, he had saved a few silver coins, a mix of Centavos and Reals, enough he hoped to get himself to El Paso City. The last item was given to him by his mother shortly before she died.

He lifted up the thin black scarf tied together with a red ribbon and inspected it. Inside was a gold coin, roughly stamped and oddly shaped. He didn't know much about it, only that his mother had it for many years and kept it with her at all times. *It will be my good luck coin,* he thought. *I will also keep it with me all the time for luck and to remember my mother.*

Garza thought about the traqueros' warnings, and about the need for a pistol. *I will be able to take care of myself,* he decided, dismissing the idea. Closing his eyes, he tried to envision his future and what he would leave behind in Zacatecas. He knew he wouldn't miss the crushing darkness and brutal labor of the silver mines. Day after day, the same routine slowly drained the life out of the workers. Accidents were common. His best friend, Jose Herrera, had been killed in a cave-in at the end of a new drift. For every worker killed or injured, there were ten more to take his place. Workers were discarded like so much trash. He thought about his friends and co-workers who had been lost to the mine, all for a little silver. All for nothing as he saw it.

He had been preparing for the trip north a long time. His mother made him learn to read his native language as a small boy. His writing was still poor, but he could sign his full name and was quite proud of it. Hector de Monte Garza Reuda sounded so formal and official to him. The name Garza was from his father, someone he never knew, and Reuda was from his mother, as was the Mexican fashion.

He had decided a long time ago that if he were to leave Mexico for the United States of America, he should learn the language. Whenever he was around anyone speaking English, he would listen and question and file away what he could. Although he was able to remember and speak many words, he still had difficulty pronouncing them. He knew this would come in time, as soon as he reached El Paso City. He also knew it was time to go. The rails led the way to his future and, as he saw it, the way to a great adventure.

Preparing himself for the trip ahead was exciting. All he could think of was El Paso City and what was ahead of him. Using one of his two real coins, he bought some extra tortillas and dried meat, as well as a few local chilies for the trip. He tucked it all safely away in a crudely made bag, fashioned from the blanket on his pallet. A strap went over one shoulder and in the bag he kept his knife and other provisions. His zarape and a short length of rope completed his modest travel kit. The silver coins and his lucky coin he kept in a small pouch around his neck, the safest place he could think of.

Standing next to the rails, he looked for a moment at the only home he'd ever known. As the train shuddered to a stop, he turned his back on Zacatecas for the last time. He slung his bag over his shoulder and climbed into the train car. Finding a seat near the rear, he strained to see out the window toward the engine. It was a filthy looking beast, with gritty black smoke and fire belching from the chimney and steam swirling all around it. The monster had taken on its fill of water and the car behind it was piled high with firewood. A few people made a last-minute rush to one of the two passenger cars, arms full of bags and one with a small child in tow. He was jarred back to reality by a man tapping him on the shoulder.

"You have a ticket señor?"

He looked up into the face of a tall heavy white man wearing a strange blue hat.

"No. But I have money, I can pay."

"What is your destination?"

"Sir?" said Garza, not understanding the man's broken Spanish.

"Your destination. How far are you going? You know, where are you getting off?"

"The United State of Texas."

"You will get off in Ciudad Juarez," said blue hat. "That will be seventy-five Centavos for your ticket."

Garza hadn't been prepared to spend so much for the trip, but he reached into his small pouch and brought out the needed coins. The conductor took the money and handed him a small piece of paper. He stared at the ticket for a moment. One side was printed in Spanish and the other in English. The official ticket to his great adventure he thought. He tucked it away in his bag with his other possessions.

The train lurched, shuddered, and began to roll forward. As they picked up speed, the acrid smoke from the engine poured in through the open windows of the car. People scrambled to pull down their windows and get away from the stench. It was stifling hot in the car and would only get worse as the day got longer, but it was the first day of his adventure and he was still excited.

As the engine labored up the steep grades and wound through the mountains, he became fascinated by every tree, valley, and rocky cliff that rolled by. He tried to imagine El Paso City and what it might hold. Never having been more than a few miles from Zacatecas, every turn showed him something new, something to be filed away in his memory.

After a few hours he pulled out a tortilla and a strip of dried meat and chewed it mindlessly, staring out the window as the Mexican panorama went by. The railroad was changing the way of life in Mexico, this much he understood. Since it arrived in Zacatecas, many new people had arrived looking for work in the mines. A few like him had left to find something better. It was the talk of the town. Every day someone had a new railroad story about what was at the end of the tracks. The people who ran the silver mines were the ones who benefitted the most. They were able to get supplies and ship their silver much faster than before.

The train pulled two cars for passengers, the last two cars before the caboose, and six others for freight. The passenger business was just a small part of the new system. They carried traqueros and employees of the railway, as well as a few paying passengers. The cars had plain, hard wooden benches for seats and passengers bounced and slid around with every sway and jerk of the train.

When the railroad finally reached Zacatecas for the first time, it had many more cars and two engines. It was decorated with Mexican and American flags and banners hung from every car. The station had been decorated with Chinese lanterns and flat earthenware bowls with floating wicks used as oil lamps. Local musicians had been pressed into service to play for the occasion and many dignitaries of the railway were in attendance. After everyone had their fill of the big event, the hundreds of people began to leave and the train lumbered out of the station with several sharp blasts of the whistle. Now the trains just came and went, routinely hauling freight and passengers in much more modest conditions.

After a few hours, Garza was startled by several blasts of the whistle and the monster shuddered to a stop for more water and wood. Everyone got off to get a drink of their own and find a place to stretch their legs and relieve themselves. He wandered the length of the train, taking in all the details. His curiosity temporarily satisfied, he climbed back into the last car and slid across the seat claiming his spot next to the window.

Eventually, the train moved out of the mountains and into flatter and more arid looking country. *This must be what the desert looks like*," he decided. Although he had never seen the desert before, this was surely what he had heard about from the traqueros. On one side of the tracks ran the telegraph wire, another recent addition brought in with the railway. The poles ran by in a smooth blur, adding a bit of drama to the otherwise boring landscape.

The train stopped in Chihuahua, a good-sized city, thought by some to be one of the most beautiful in this part of Mexico. After they ground to a stop, he could see that the town was laid out with a small square and a fountain surrounded by walks and streets lined with many trees

"Pardon señor, may I sit here?"

He looked up to see a young Mexican man, slightly older than him with a large straw hat in his hand and a bag over his shoulder. Garza moved his bag from the seat and motioned for him to sit.

"Thank you. I am Angel Lopez. I am traveling to El Paso Del Norte for work."

Heck introduced himself and settled in for the long ride and Lopez fell immediately to sleep.

*

The train's whistle jarred Heck awake. Lopez was still sound asleep with a firm grip on his bag and his straw hat down over his eyes. After many stops and many more hours, the train had arrived in El Paso Del Norte, the Mexican sister to El Paso, Texas. The Rio Grande River rolled sluggishly between the two siblings. *More like a slow-moving puddle than a great river,* thought Heck.

The train blew its whistle again and rolled to a stop in front of a small adobe building that served as a passenger station and a maintenance shop for the traqueros. "All Mexican citizens off the train now!" hollered the conductor. Lopez sat straight up and looked to the front of the car. "What are we doing now?"

"You are getting off the train — now!" said the conductor. "You must show your documents to the authorities if you want to cross into El Paso." The two men got off the train, looking around at the station and the rough streets surrounding them.

They walked a few hundred yards and found a spot to sit under the shade of a large Cottonwood above the river. Lopez was taller than Garza and at least twenty pounds heavier. Outgoing and talkative, he was much the opposite of Heck. He could make friends with anyone. Though his English was not great, he had a way of making himself understood to everyone he met. He had one unique quality that he had never seen before, the ability to fall asleep within a minute, whenever and wherever he wanted. Heck thought this seemed like a good trait to have, as he often lay awake for hours before falling to sleep.

As the two men talked, they realized they both wanted the same things, a better life and a great adventure. Lopez came from Tampico, near the east coast of Mexico. "I was from a family of fishermen. My father, my brother, and I had a small boat," said Angel. "When my father got very old and could not fish any longer, my brother and I fished alone. When my father died, my brother went to work on a larger boat and I went to work for a horse farm for two years. But I always wondered what Texas was like, so here I am."

After a meal, they came to an agreement. They would stick together for now until each found something they liked. Until then they would watch out for each other day and night. That day they made another decision. Since neither had papers of any kind and no family to worry about, they would cross into El Paso City after dark and see what their fortunes had waiting for them.

An overcast night made it easy to slip around the bridge and cross the river. When they came up on a small rise, they saw a sea of dull flickering lights. They sprinted to the first row of buildings and dropped down behind a short adobe wall. The nights were still cold and both put on their zerapes and lay down out of the wind. Before he could say anything, his new amigo was sleeping soundly.

*

With the sun filtering through the shapes he saw last night, he opened his eyes slowly. He realized they were on the edge of a wide jumble of adobe huts, mostly low buildings threaded through with rough dusty streets. Angel still slept soundly against the wall with his head on his bag and the straw hat down over his face.

In a moment he sat up with his eyes wide open and surveying his surroundings. "What now, señor Heck? Shall we make our way into town?"

Before he could respond, a long shadow appeared to move toward them. Stopping a few steps away was a short stocky man in a baggy black shirt and gray pants. He wore a small form fitting cap and sported a long single pigtail half way down his back. They both instantly recognized the stranger as a Chinaman, one of thousands who migrated to America through Mexico. This unusual looking character stared at them for the longest time before speaking.

He thought how odd it was that he learned English in preparation for his trip to El Paso City and the first person they ran into spoke a language he had never heard before. For the next few minutes, through gestures and sounds, the stranger understood that they needed something to drink and eat. The strange little man turned and motioned for them to follow. They walked with him through the maze of adobes and narrow winding streets and into the door of a long narrow adobe house.

As their eyes adjusted slowly to the light of a single lamp, the travelers saw two children and one woman gathered in the back of the room. After a short conversation, the oldest of the children, a boy of about fifteen or sixteen, came forward and spoke in Spanish. "I am Wang Po Ching, this is my father Wang Dau, my mother Wang Mei Ling and my sister Wang Shan-Shan," said the boy. "Would you like something to drink and eat?"

Heck nodded his head, surprised at hearing his native language spoken so well. "Thank you. We would like that very much. How is it that you speak such good Spanish?"

"My father says that I need to learn the local languages so that we may fit in and find a life in this country." The boy motioned for them to sit on the floor.

"Do you speak English also?"

"I am learning, but it is coming much more slowly than the local Spanish," said Wang Po.

They ate quickly and quietly while the family gathered around. Each member of the family gave a small bow or slight dip of the head when introduced. The guests each introduced themselves, not knowing that a fast friendship was being forged in this dimly lit room on the outskirts of El Paso.

Angel was talking a mile a minute to Wang Po. They seemed to bond instantly. It was as though they couldn't wait to get the words out. The young man appeared to understand a little about everything. Farming, horses, cattle, and local politics were just some of the issues they talked about. He listened intently, occasionally asking a question. Taking in all the information, he filed it away for future use.

The Wang home was about fifteen feet wide and twenty-five feet long. The walls were made of adobe bricks, plastered on the inside and covered with a thick whitewash. Next to the door was a small window, and in the back was a fireplace built into the corner. Across from the fireplace was a ladder leading up through a small opening into another room above. It was a tiny, unheated space with another small window in the front, used as a sleeping room by the whole family. It was one of only a few of the modest houses that had an additional room above. A small white statue of Budda sat on a shelf above the fireplace, and a few candles and two colorful lanterns were hanging from the ceiling.

This rough plain house was home for the family and now for their invited guests. By the time they had finished the meal and the conversation had slowed, the day was gone and Wang Dau had invited them to stay the night. Thanking their hosts, they threw their zerapes down in front of the fireplace and settled in. The events of the day swirled around in his head so fast that he lay in front of the fire several hours before falling asleep.

In the morning, the house became a rush of activity. Mei Ling had cooked a breakfast meal while Po Ching and his father were preparing to go to work. As they left the house, Heck and Angel followed them through the maze and onto a wide road with a lot of traffic. A few minutes later they stopped in front of the slaughter plant where they worked. Po Ching pointed down the road to the west and told them that was the main part of the town. He also advised them to be cautious. "El Paso is a very dangerous place. Be very careful and please come to our home tonight."

They nodded, thanked their new friends, and started down the road to the famous town. As they walked alongside the road, they were amazed at the steady stream of carriages, freight wagons, horses, cattle, sheep, and goats that mixed with the people moving along the rutted road. Dogs seemed to have the run of the town, running through the legs of the horses pulling the wagons. There seemed to be no end to the traffic and new things to take in.

Reaching the center of town, they saw the train station and many different sets of tracks with several cars and engines waiting in a lazy cloud of smoke and steam. People came and went, carriages and coaches of all kinds were loading and unloading people, and trains were constantly blowing their whistles. Teamsters backed their wagons up to the landing and men moved freight in and out of the cars. Some were handling freight from the mines at Zacatecas, already a rapidly fading memory in his young mind. Everything and everyone were covered in a fine layer of dust from all the activity.

The two new Texicans, as they had decided to call themselves, walked past the activity at the train station and onto the main street of the city. Saloons and gambling casinos were on every block, with an occasional hotel, café, or Chinese laundry wedged between the businesses. The non-stop activity of the scene excited the two young men.

"Have you seen anything else like this before?" asked Angel.

"Once, when the train finally came to my village, but even that was not as busy as here."

The dirt roads were nothing but ruts and clouds of fine dust. Two wagons with water tanks on them, pulled by giant draft horses sprayed water in the streets in a futile attempt to keep the dust down. People darted in and out of the traffic, as though they were all in some kind of odd concert with each other. Rough, dirty-looking men mingled with well-dressed businessmen and even rougher looking women. It was a lot to take in for their first day, but he found everything he saw exciting.

They found their way back through the maze to their new friends' house and found Mei Ling stirring her large round pot over the fire. She was cutting meat into small pieces, dropping them in the pan while she stirred. Po Ching smiled when he saw them and immediately picked up his conversation with Angel where they left off that morning.

Listening to the conversation during the evening meal, Heck noticed Shan-Shan, the daughter of the family, sitting quietly to the side. Looking closely at her for the first time as the candle light flickered off the walls, he realized just how beautiful this young Chinese girl was. She had a natural, fragile kind of beauty with flawless pale skin and mysterious dark eyes that seemed to shine through the low light.

Shan-Shan was about a year younger than her brother and only spoke Chinese. She and her mother took in some laundry in their home for extra money, but she never left the house on her own.

They spent several days with the family, looking for work during the daylight hours, and helping with things around the modest house. By the end of the third day, Heck was totally transfixed by her. It was the first time he'd ever felt anything like this. As far as he was concerned, he now saw his life laid out before him, a life with Shan-Shan as his wife.

The Bride

For the new Texicans, the days in El Paso City were a constant blur. Angel had some experience with animals and quickly found work at a livery on the edge of town. He worked six days a week and found the work easy enough, but the days were long and tiring. When he was paid, he walked through town with the money in his pocket and his hand wrapped tightly around it. The temptations to spend it immediately were everywhere. So far he had sampled very little.

Once a week, he bought two pieces of the hard candy displayed in the window of a local dry goods store. He'd never tasted anything so sweet before.

Heck found work at the railroad depot loading and unloading freight. He also contributed to the family kitchen but never spent any money beyond that. Each night they returned to the family's home, after the meal they gathered in front of the fireplace and talked of their past and what they all hoped for the future. He already knew what his future would be, he just had to decide how to ask for Shan-Shan's hand.

After several weeks, it was obvious to everyone in the house that Shan-Shan felt the same way he did. They were always looking at each other, smiling and sharing a quick touch when they thought no one else was looking. She would brush against him and touch his hand whenever she had the chance. Several times she gave a squeeze to his fingers or touched his hair. Heck thought about her all day during work and watched her as she moved and worked around the house.

*

At the loading dock, his boss, an older silver-haired man named Cesar, also from Zacatecas, took him aside one day shortly before the end of his shift. "Heck, do you want to stay in the United States?"

"Very much señor ."

"I have been asked to find good workers that would like to move North with the railroad to the New Mexico Territory. You are a hard worker. I would not like to see you go, but you will have a better chance for success up there."

He thought about this offer for several minutes before he answered. "And this territory is in the United States?"

"Right now, the territory of New Mexico is owned by the United States, but they say it will be a state very soon. There will be much opportunity for a young hard worker such as yourself."

"I would have some business to attend to before I left, would that be permissible?"

"It would, but don't wait too many days. There are others that would go if they knew about it."

"Gracias, señor, I will be back tomorrow and you can give me the information."

*

Sitting in front of the fireplace with the family, he nervously wondered how to tell Wang Dau what was on his mind. Finally, his nerves got the best of him and he suddenly blurted out, "Wang Dau, I want to marry your daughter — Shan-Shan — your daughter — I want to marry her!"

Po Ching burst out laughing. "We were all wondering when you would find the courage to say something," he said, still laughing.

"What do you mean?"

"Everyone has watched you two making eyes at each other for weeks. Even father and mother knew what was happening."

Looking embarrassed, he wanted to know if he would please just ask his father for permission. "Of course." When he finished talking, his father grinned, nodded his head, and bowed. "It's official, Shan-Shan will be your bride."

Wang Dau motioned for his daughter to come and sit next to him. After a few minutes of quiet conversation, she looked at Heck, nodded her head, and gave a small bow. The wedding was officially approved by everyone.

"Mister Heck," said Po Ching, "the wedding will be tomorrow night. Mother is sad that Shan-Shan will not have a real traditional Chinese wedding, but she would like you to agree to do a few things for the ceremony."

"Just tell me what it is, and I will do it."

"You must give Shan-Shan a wedding gift. It does not have to be anything fancy, but something special to you."

"That's all?"

"No, you must pay the father for the bride."

"Pay him what? I have very little . . ."

"How much is not important. We all have very little. But again, a small token, perhaps a coin or two if you have it. Also, do not come back to the house until dark and bring something sweet for the banquet. Mother will spend the day in preparation with her daughter."

The next morning he told his supervisor about the wedding. He explained he would be ready to leave for the New Mexico Territory tomorrow.

"That will be fine. Be here early and you will ride the train to your new job. You have not asked what the job is."

"It does not matter. I can do whatever it may be."

That day he spent several hours moving freight. At noon his supervisor told him to go and prepare for his wedding. "I will see you and your bride when the sun comes up."

Heck walked through the streets of El Paso, wondering what he would get for gifts. As he passed by the saloons and livery stables, he came to a small bakery advertising fresh bread. The smells coming through the door were unlike anything he had experienced before. Walking into the store, a man greeted him from the back room. "Buenos tardes, señor. How can I help you today?"

"Tell me, please, what is that wonderful smell?"

"That would be my special sweet bread. I make it with sugar and cinnamon for the cowboys. They like to have something sweet tasting out in the lonely desert. It gets hard quickly, so it keeps very well. Would you like a taste?"

"Si." He held the bread in his mouth for a moment, savoring the unique flavor. "How much would a loaf of this special bread cost?"

"Five centavos. Enough for several people to enjoy. If you keep it for a while, it will get hard, as I said. But if you heat it or soak it in milk or coffee, it will be good again."

"Please give me two of the loaves."

As the sun began to set over the hills, it gave him an idea. He was now prepared to marry.

*

He stood at the front door of Wang Dau's house as the last light disappeared. He was scared for the first time in his life. His great adventure was moving along faster than he ever thought possible. Knocking on the door, he shuffled his feet and wiped his forehead with his scarf. When the door opened, he took a deep breath and stepped inside.

Po Ching sat on the floor next to his father. Several new lanterns had been hung and a clean white cloth had been laid out for the banquet. A curtain was hung in the back of the home as a dressing area for Shan-Shan.

"Sit here, my friend," said Po Ching. "My sister will be here in a few moments; mother is helping her prepare now. This place is for you. Shan-Shan will sit between you and father. Did you bring the gifts?"

"I have them. Should I give them to him now?"

"Give father his now."

He handed him a small tin can. Wrapped inside of it with a piece of red ribbon was a newly minted United States silver dollar. As he handed it to him, he gave him a small bow and sat back down. He opened it slowly. When he held it up, he smiled broadly and nodded.

"You have done well, Father is pleased." He said something to his son and walked to the dressing area. A moment later his mother stepped out from behind the curtain with Shan-Shan on her arm.

Angel tapped him on the arm. "Don't just sit there like a bump, stand up . . ."

Heck stood up on shaky legs. He was having trouble catching his breath and his hands shook as bad as his legs. Backlit by the colored lanterns, Shan-Shan appeared to shimmer softly, her long red dress showing off her slim figure. She had a wide blue sash at her waist and wore a blue headpiece with Chinese characters sewn on it. He didn't remember her beautiful black hair being so long, it hung well past her waist.

Unable to say anything, he couldn't stop looking at her smooth skin and dark eyes. *This could not be,* he thought. *Surely this is not really happening to me . . .*

The rest of the ceremony was a haze for Heck. He heard the words and ate the meal, but he never took his eyes off of his new bride. When it ended, he had to be reminded again about the gift for Shan-Shan. He remembered the sweet bread and sat a loaf on the cloth, asking Po Ching to explain it to the family. After they all tried it, he handed a small black cloth tied with a red ribbon to her. She opened it slowly, the look of excitement filling her face. It was a small gold coin, a type that none of them had ever seen before. Leaning forward she showed it to her mother and father. Obviously pleased, they smiled and nodded repeatedly to him. She wrapped the coin back up and clutched it tightly for the rest of the evening.

As the evening wound down, her father whispered something to her. They both nodded and Shan-Shan took his hand and led him to the ladder. They would spend their first night alone in the family's sleeping room. Nothing else was said by anyone. Angel added wood to the fire and everyone lay down on the floor for the evening.

In the dim light of several lanterns, Heck could see the sleeping room had a fresh clean pallet with extra blankets. Shan-Shan motioned for him to sit down. She stood in front of him bathed in the flickering light, the red of her dress glowing softly through the darkness. After removing her headpiece, she shook out her hair and released the sash around her waist. Stepping out of the dress, she lay it aside and watched his eyes.

Heck could hardly breathe. He had never even been close to a woman as beautiful as this. Staring at his new wife, he thought about everything that had happened in just a few weeks. He had left his home and the misery that was the silver mine, and now he had a beautiful wife standing in front of him. He was so nervous that for a moment he thought he might be sick. His hands shook and his heart pounded wildly.

Shan-Shan reached out and caressed his face. Sitting down next to him she nodded, touching his sleeve and looking at him. She touched it again and motioned at the pallet. Suddenly he understood what she meant. As he started to undress, she lay on the bed watching him. He had never seen a naked woman before, let alone been naked in front of one himself.

Turning to face her, his emotions took over and he began to cry. She took his shaking hand in hers and kissed it, then kissed him on the lips. Wiping his tears away, she kissed him again and gently pulled him onto the pallet next to her. They lay together touching and kissing each other's bodies. The warmth of her soft skin against his chest and her hair cascading all around him was almost more than he could take. They spent the night locked in each other's arms, neither wanting to let go.

After the morning meal everyone said their goodbyes to the new husband and wife. They each carried their modest possessions in a homemade shoulder bag. Shan-Shan's mother made one for her daughter out of the same red and blue fabric her wedding dress was made from. As the last of the tears were shed, the new couple stepped outside the home and looked back one more time and waved. Then they turned to head to the rail station.

"Wait, one more minute, I am coming with you," said Angel, "at least to the station."

"Thank you, my friend. We would like the company."

Walking through the rows of adobe houses, they talked about what they had been through in such a short time and what the future might have for them. "I would like to have a small ranch someday," said Angel. "Maybe a few sheep and some cows. A garden would be good also. Do you know what you will do for the railroad when you get to the New Mexico territory?"

"I didn't ask, I know I can do whatever they give me."

"Where will you and Shan-Shan live when you get there?"

"I was told that there will be a room for us. It will be in one of the traqueros camps, but will be good for now."

As they walked, Shan-Shan held his arm tightly. Dressed in drab pants and shirt, with a black cloth cap pulled down low, she had her hair in a long Chinese pigtail. Po Ching had cautioned him to always keep her close. "Men in this place can be very cruel," he said. "She will always draw a lot of attention; you must keep her safe."

Reaching the already smoking train, he hugged Angel. "Take care my friend. I will write the family a letter when I get time and tell you where we are."

"Have a good adventure. We will meet again, of this I'm sure."

New Citizens

Sitting close together they held each other's hand tightly. It was Shan-Shan's first time on a train and she was amazed at how fast the countryside went by, and by the noise and shaking going on. Unable to speak each other's language, they stayed like this until the first water stop. When he pointed to her and the platform asking if she wanted to get off, she shook her head and tightened her grip.

The next stop was the small town of Las Cruces. This time they had to get off and find the stationmaster and give him his letter of introduction. "You will go to the traqueros camp and check in with Squeak. He will tell you where to go from there."

"Squeak? That is his name?"

"It is. Don't ask me why, 'cause I don't care."

Surprised by his abrupt nature, they walked hand in hand to the camp and asked the first man they saw for Squeak. He pointed to a wagon loaded with gravel. There was only one man near the wagon and he walked over, stuck out his hand, and introduced himself. "I am Heck, this is my wife Shan-Shan. I have this letter about a job for you to look at."

The man looked at the letter. "This is for a position in Socorro, north of here about a hundred and fifty miles or so. You need to get back on the train and stay on until they stop at the Socorro station. Then give the letter to the stationmaster, a fellow named Dutch." The train shook and rumbled for several more hours, pulling into the station just before dark. They asked for Dutch at the station counter. "I'm Dutch, what can I do for you?"

"I am Heck, and this is my wife Shan-Shan. I have a letter about a railroad job here."

"What did they tell you about a place to stay?"

"They said we would be in the worker's camp."

"Well shit — goddamnit they do this every time!"

"Do what sir?"

"Send me a new hire and never ask if I have a place for them to stay. On top of that, you have a wife, shit — goddamnit anyway . . . well, come with me."

The camp was a long row of adobe huts with common walls between them. "Wait here." He walked into the room on the end and they began to hear two men arguing. In a minute a short, dirty man came out with Dutch behind him. "This is yours for now. I'd suggest you clean that bed before you sleep in it."

"Where will that man sleep?"

"He'll find a place with somebody else or he'll sleep outside. There's a stove for cooking, a bed, a skillet, and a pot. Get your water from the creek. You are responsible for your own food, the privies are out back. Be at the station at sunup."

"Thank you sir," said Heck, peering inside.

"Oh, and a piece of advice for you, young man. Keep a close eye on that pretty wife of yours, 'specially around these men."

The room a low ceiling and one small window next to the door. In the back wall, up high, was a second window that had a board covering it. The smell of wood smoke and general filth of a dozen workers before them hung in the air. A table, two chairs, and a narrow wood-frame bed nearly filled the room.

Shan-Shan stood in the entrance looking at their first home. Walking in, she motioned for him to follow. Grabbing the bedding by the corner, she pulled it off the bed and threw it out the door. Handing the pot to him, she motioned for him to fill it with water. When he returned with the water, the chairs and table were outside the door and the front window was wide open. Pointing to the back window she motioned for him remove the board. When he cleared the window, he could see why it was boarded up. The glass had been broken out.

Before he could set the water down, she pointed to the stove and motioned to the wood next to it. "You are a bossy little woman, aren't you?" he said, knowing she didn't understand. She pointed at the stove and the wood again and looked at him. He nodded his head. "Maybe you do understand me . . ."

When the water began to boil, Shan-Shan soaked a rag in it and began to clean the bed frame. Taking his hand, she walked him out the door and pointed to the bedding and the blanket. Raising her arm above her head and swung it down toward the bedding. He looked confused for a moment and she repeated the motion several more times. In frustration she picked up the corner of the blanket and hit it several times. Seeing the dust come off the blanket, he realized what she was trying to say. He grinned at her and nodded his head.

Walking to a row of bushes, he spread the bedding across them, found a substantial stick and began to beat them until no more dust came out. After doing both sides twice, he folded them up and brought them back to the room. Setting them on the bed frame, he watched his new bride work. She pointed to him and the bedding then touched the bare bed.

When she leaned over, he tried to pull her close for a kiss and she straightened up. Again, she pointed to the bedding and then at him. He smiled and tried once more and again she pulled away. This time he thought he detected a small smile before she began to point. Grabbing the bedding, he spread it out and put the blanket on top along with the extra blanket they brought with them. When he finished, he pointed to the bed and looked at her. Checking it out, she nodded her approval, broke into a smile and pulled him onto the bed.

*

In the morning, he tried his best to explain to her that she needed to stay in the house until he returned. He showed her how to wedge the door shut from the inside and laid in some more firewood and another pot of water. She still had a little food in her bag and two small cups that her mother had given her, several pairs of chopsticks and three rice bowls. She also had two tin plates and a small knife given to her by her brother.

Heck's first day was busy but boring. The whole morning was spent moving railroad ties from one pile to another. When they got the ties relocated, the supervisor had them shovel gravel into large freight wagons. The wagons were then backed up on a ramp next to the open train car. The rest of the day was spent shoveling gravel from the wagons into the train car.

Tired and dirty, he stopped at the creek to wash up. Walking home he stopped at the company supply store and spent a nickel on a stiff scrub brush and ten cents on a broom. He found a bolt of blue and white cloth with only a few feet of fabric left and asked the shopkeeper how much. "Ain't all that much left there. Call it five cents and you can have it."

Picking up a ball of heavy twine, he sat it next to the brush. "How much more?"

"Three cents. Will that be all you need?"

As he pulled the coins from his pouch, he noticed a jar with dark colored hard candy inside. As he was looking at it the man reached in, grabbed two pieces, and handed them to him. "Usually I get a penny for two pieces, but now that you're a good customer, these are on me."

"Muchas gracias, señor. I will be back again as soon as I get paid."

Pushing on the door, he found the lock he had fashioned was not in place. When his eyes adjusted to the light, he saw Shan-Shan on her hands and knees scrubbing the wood floor with a wet rag. When she saw him, she stood up and gave him a kiss on the cheek. He looked around the room and was shocked to see what she had accomplished. Three of the four walls had been completely washed and the adobe showed the original light brown color. The ceiling, the stove, and the furniture had been washed down and the table was set with the plates and cups from her mother.

He had to stop for a moment to take it all in. The most surprising thing was both windows had small white curtains over them. The top corners of the curtains were tucked into a crack in the adobe but looked good. He'd forgotten the supplies in his hand until she started to tug at the broom handle. When she saw the broom and the brush, she bowed slightly, placing them in the corner. The cloth made her smile and bow again, but this time she hugged him and kissed him on the mouth.

Holding the ball of twine, she seemed to wonder what it was for. "It's for a clothesline. You know, to hang things up?"

When it was obvious she didn't know, he took one end and fastened it to the front window frame and pulled it across the room to the back one. She instantly understood. Grabbing her cleaning rag, she draped it over the twine and nodded her head. They now had a clothesline. Leading him to the table she motioned to gather up the plates and bowls. Within a few minutes she had the new blue and white cloth folded to fit the table and she motioned to him to replace the tableware.

When they were ready to go to bed, he showed her what else he had purchased, two pieces of hard candy. He broke one in two and gave her the first taste. Her eyes lit up and she smiled and nodded her head several times. She bent over and kissed him again and again. He fell into bed with her and they made love several times. He would remember to have plenty of candy with him at all times.

After the second day of work, he bathed quickly in the nearby stream and walked up to his front door. Pushing on it, he found it unlocked again. Stepping inside he could hardly believe what he was seeing. The room was completely cleaned and the windows now had curtains that matched the tablecloth. The clothesline had been secured at both ends and the skillet had something cooking in it. In the middle of the table was a discarded red coffee can with several different wildflowers in it.

Although his bride did a remarkable job on the ancient adobe, it was obvious that she had been in and out several times that day, and this worried him. He needed to get her to understand the dangers and the language barrier was making it impossible. The next day he asked if any of the other workers knew how to speak Chinese, or knew someone who did. His supervisor told him that he had much the same problem, and if either of them found someone, they might be able to help both of them.

He heard about a man in another part of the camp who had a Chinese wife and walked through the camp on Sunday looking for him. What he found was a tall, very fat Mexican man, much different than the typical slim Mexican track worker. He was named Reynaldo and was married to an older Chinese woman. They had four kids with them in the small apartment and Heck found him sitting on a bench outside.

"Si, my wife is Chinese and can also speak Spanish and English," said the man. "I'm sure she could help you. Rosa — come out here!"

"Your Chinese wife is called Rosa?"

"That's what I call her, I can't say her Chinese name." She was a pleasant looking woman with gray hair pulled back tight and a large smile. "Rosa, this man has a Chinese wife that does not yet speak English. He would like you to help him."

She nodded her head. "Si, señor, I can help."

"Thank you. When can I bring her by so that I don't interrupt your day?"

"Ha! Please interrupt my day any time you want. I will shoo the kids out and we will have a meal and I will help you all I can. What are your names?"

"I am Heck and my wife is Shan-Shan. Thank you again for your offer. We will be by after supper tomorrow if this is good?"

"As I said, anytime is good, I will make my fat husband go outside with the kids and leave us alone."

*

They walked hand in hand to Rosa's home. Reynaldo greeted them from his bench. He had a large cigar in his mouth, a real extravagance for a track worker. "Go on in, she's waiting for you." As they opened the door, a cluster of little bodies poured outside and disappeared down the road.

"I'm so glad you are here. I am cooking rice with fish and tortillas."

"Will your husband be eating with us?"

"My fat husband has already been fed. He'll be on that bench until he comes to bed after dark. Shan-Shan? Did I get that correct?" She asked in perfect Mandarin.

It was the first time she had heard the language since she left her father's house and she had forgotten how much she missed it. "Yes, you are correct. What is your Chinese name?"

"My name is Hasio, though he has always called me Rosa because he cannot pronounce it."

He listened to them talk in Chinese while she prepared the food. He was glad Shan-Shan had someone to talk with. "Rosa, I am concerned that she does not understand how much danger there is for a young woman in this camp. I am afraid that something bad will happen when I'm not here."

"Not to worry señor, I will explain things to her. Now let's eat and we will talk after."

The women talked for several hours, only pausing occasionally for Rosa to explain to him what they were talking about. When it was time to leave, Rosa hugged them and told him that she would love to help her learn. "When you go to work, you bring her here and then you pick her up on your way home, okay? That way she will be safe and she can learn."

He took Shan-Shan's hand and asked her if she would like that, Rosa translated. She looked at him, smiled broadly and nodded.

"Gracias Señora, I will have her here in the morning."

*

Rosa was a good teacher and had Shan-Shan speaking many of the basic English words within a few weeks. "She is very smart and a very fast learner," said Rosa when he came to get her. "She is very excited to learn as much as she can as quickly as she can. Sometimes I must ask her to slow down her questions. Be sure to talk with her as much as you can at home, it will help."

Sitting on the bed, he reached over to turn down the lamp and Shan-Shan stopped him. "No, please . . ."

It was the first time that he ever heard her say anything in English and it sounded perfect. She took his hands in hers and looked in his eyes. "Heck — okay, Heck?"

"Yes, Heck, Heck is okay."

"Heck, Heck. Love — Heck — okay?"

Grabbing her and pulling her close, he kissed her again and again. "Si, I mean, yes — I love you too . . ."

Every night she brought home at least two new words, and they practiced in the evenings while lying in bed. As her English began to improve, they started to mix in a few Spanish words. She wanted to know how a Chinese word for something was spoken in both other languages. After learning a little Spanish, she teased him, calling him *mi señor poco* (my little mister).

"You are doing very well. We are now New Mexicans and very soon New Mexico will become a state, and we will be two new Americans in the United State of New Mexico."

She shook her head at his statement. "No. Please — no. Not two Americans — please . . ."

"What is wrong? You don't want to be an American?"

"No — not two Americans . . ."

"I don't understand, talk slower."

She looked at him for a moment then smiled and kissed him gently, "Not two Americans. Yes — tres — Americans."

He still didn't understand what she was trying to tell him.

106

"Three Americans? What do you mean three?"

She could hardly contain her huge grin. "Tres — three Americans?"

When he finally understood what she was saying he stood up and stared at her. "Bebe? Si? Bebe?"

His face flushed and his hands began to shake. "Bebe? Yes — baby?"

"Yes, baby — bebe — three Americans . . ."

Magdalena

After months of moving ties, gravel and rails at the yard, his supervisor called him into the shack used as an office. "Heck, how is your wife feeling? I know she is expecting a child."

"She is well."

"How is her English coming along?"

"She speaks very well. Has Rosa been helping your wife too?"

"Yes, but she takes to it very slowly. Heck, I am very glad to have you working for me here in Socorro. You are my hardest worker. But now I have to ask you something. I am leaving the railroad soon, to go back to Texas and care for my sister. That leaves my job open for a new supervisor. There is also a new position in the town of Magdalena, to the west of here, for a new station master. Before I leave, I have to pick someone for both jobs. Which one would you like?"

He sat quietly, trying to take in this new information. "You want me to be a supervisor? I have never done that before."

"I know you would be a fine supervisor. You know the job here. It is mostly hard labor and long boring hours. I think you should consider the position in Magdalena; it is for a station master. It is a small town but is on the end of our newest spur line. You will not have to build track, just run the station. Things will be very slow at first, then growing fast in the next few years. Right now, most of their business is shipping livestock to Socorro. I believe it will be an exciting place for a young man starting out. You will be in charge of everything sent on the train, and you can run it any way you think is best."

This was the second time he had been offered a better job since he started with the railroad. His head was spinning with questions about everything, but he knew it would have to be okay with Shan-Shan before he could give an answer. "If I were to be the supervisor there, where would we live?"

"There is a house built just for the station master not far from the station. I have been there once, and it is clean and large enough for a small family."

"I have to talk to my wife, but I will give you the answer tomorrow."

"Very good, we will talk tomorrow."

Shan-Shan asked no questions and agreed to the move immediately. "A new adventure is good. Our baby will still be born in America, I like that."

*

They loaded their modest possessions into a trunk and stepped up into the passenger car. The supervisor handed him an envelope. "Here is the letter for the station master. He is in a hurry to leave, so find him right away. I have already sent him a telegraph that you are coming. Muchas gracias my friend, and take care."

The ride to Magdalena was short and mostly through the dry lands. They watched the mountains go by on their left as the engine pulled the train up the gentle incline. When they got to Magdalena, they were surprised at the activity. Since the arrival of the railroad, the town had become a center of shipping for ore, timber, cattle, and sheep. Dozens of cattle pens sat off to the side of the rail yard and cowboys were in the pens working the cows on horseback.

Cattle and sheep had been driven from all over western New Mexico and Arizona for years on a trail known as the cattle driveway. The driveway, a long stretch of desolate country, came from Springerville, Arizona and was used to drive thousands of cattle and sheep east every year. Ranches along the way moved their stock onto the driveway and drove them to Socorro. The new Magdalena spur became the destination for tens of thousands of head of livestock. Dozens of railcars sat on the sidings waiting to be loaded. Just past the cattle were more pens filled with thousands of sheep waiting to be loaded.

They walked into the depot and he asked where he could find the station master, a man named Reeves. "He's around somewhere. That's his house out back," said the clerk, pointing through the window. "He wears a wide straw hat."

The front door opened before he could knock. "You would be Heck?"

"I am. We have come for the new job."

"Well, this house is yours now, here are the keys to the depot and the office. Let's go there now and I'll show you everything. The back room of the depot was small and cluttered with piles of papers and boxes. Two wooden file cabinets were alongside the desk, each with its own key. On the opposite wall was a large black safe, nearly four feet tall with double doors. It had ornate gold stripes and a picture of a stream and trees painted on the door. Below the picture was the name *Magdalena, New Mexico*. The name above the door, also in gold, said *Atchison Topeka & Santa Fe Railway*.

"I will open it for you and we can inventory the contents together. Then I will lock it and give you the combinations. It takes two different ones."

Reeves went through everything in the station with him. There were two clerks working in the cage and a small room for the telegraph office with one operator. Walking toward the docks, he waved over a cowboy and introduced him as Chance Patton. At six foot five, he was easily two hundred and fifty pounds and rough looking. A thick, bushy moustache covered his whole mouth, nearly down to his chin. Heavy chaps, high heel boots with spurs and a wide brimmed hat completed the picture of the New Mexico cowboy.

"This is the new station master, Heck, uh — I don't know your last name yet. It doesn't matter anyway. He's the new me.

Starting today you work for Heck on the procedures for shipping the cattle. I'm leaving in two days for Socorro and the next day for Chicago, some place with civilized people."

"Really hate to see you go," said Patton.

"No, you don't. Let's not bullshit each other. I can't stand you and you can't stand me. Heck, this man has been a pain in my ass since I got here, now he will be a pain in your ass."

Patton laughed and put out his giant hand, squeezing hard. "I think we'll get along together just fine, don't you?"

Looking up at the figure on the horse, Heck pulled back his hand. "We will get along."

Walking back to the station, Reeves had a few more things to tell him. "Some advice for you, Heck. You're young and the workers here will try to push you around, particularly Chance. He is very good at what he does, but like most of them he will try to get away with anything he can if you let him. Never let those under you try and run your business.

You can listen to their ideas but you make all the decisions and you have to be firm. Never back down from them in an argument. Patton is a railroad employee and you are his boss. The cowboys are not railroad employees. He hires them as day workers to handle the stock as needed. He signs their time slip which they bring to the teller's cage to get paid. We also hire a few whites, Mexicans, and Chinese to work at the station if we need extra help.

"What about Indians?"

"We have used Indians before, but not too many of them come to town looking for work."

"Do the cowboys do other work around here?"

"No, they don't seem to want to get off of their horses. Trust me, you will learn about cowboys soon enough."

"One more thing, there is a Winchester rifle behind the file cabinets and a box of cartridges in the desk. You should learn to use it and keep it handy. It might be good if you had a small pistol to carry in your pocket too."

*

The house was a square, white-washed wood-frame building. It set back about two-hundred yards from the station and was the common style the railroad provided for their station masters at the newer sites. A four-hole wood burning stove was against the wall on one end, the first either of them had ever seen. A fireplace was on the opposite end and each wall had a window with plain white curtains. Shan-Shan opened the door and motioned for him to go out. "Go out now, go to your work, I stay here."

After a thorough inspection of the station with Reeves, they went over procedures and talked to the clerk on duty and telegraph operator, a young man named Red. "Railroad business takes priority on the wire," said Reeves. "Everyone else pays by the word. Red does all the paperwork and keeps the telegram money in the safe. He also handles shipping the mail for the post office. Once a week an accountant from Socorro comes and takes care of the books and takes the paperwork and extra cash. All you have to do is keep the records of money coming in and money going out."

"What about shipping the stock?"

"Chance takes care of everything from the time the cattle come off the driveway until the loaded freight cars roll out. Like I said, don't let him get away with anything. Always keep an eye on the head count. When the herd comes in, two cowboys from the ranch count them as they go into the pens. Chance counts them also, and if the numbers match, that's what the ranchers will be paid for from the buyers in Socorro."

"What about the sheep?"

"The pastores take care of everything. They do the counting and the loading themselves. They bring the counts to the cage and we handle it the same way as the cattle. The mines bring in their ore and follow the same procedure as the pastores, except the pay is determined at the other end. When the cars are loaded, we wire Socorro it's ready. They wire us back to let us know when the train can leave."

After several hours Heck was beginning to understand the basic flow of work. "It takes all of your time to keep up with this?"

"That's why the house is so close, you always have to be nearby. You'll catch on quickly, it's pretty routine. Do it the way you think is best. Thursday is the auditor's day. He'll help you understand the bookkeeping a little better."

"I can do this. I will make it the best station for the railroad."

"Well good luck with that, I wish you well."

*

In just months, he had gone from a railroad laborer to a station master. He knew that it was the AT&SF's smallest station on a dead-end spur, but he also knew that it had to grow, just like the rest of the West. He had been working on his reading, writing, and math skills since he got to New Mexico. Red volunteered to come over in the evenings to help him, and in return Shan-Shan would make them all a good meal.

He got along with the mine owners, and the Mexican pastores very well. However, the cowboys would have nothing to do with him. He understood what Reeves meant about the cowboys, they tended to be independent-minded and hardheaded. They were extremely good at caring for cattle and moving them from the pens into the cars. These dayworkers came and went as they pleased and were paid in cash every day. They waited until the big herds showed up at the station and just turned up at the pens as needed.

The cowboys that worked directly for the ranches and drove the cattle across the prairie to the pens seemed to him to be of a different temperament. They tended to be quieter and more polite and businesslike than the dayworkers and usually didn't spend any time in town, except on the Saturday night after they were paid.

The Saturday night transformation of the ranch cowboys started somewhere between the second and third drink. They came into town on their best behavior wearing their best clothes, looking for a poker table, a girl, a whisky, a fight, or all of them. They usually found everything they wanted in a short time.

After a few hours, they began to realize they might not be the toughest guys in town and end up sleeping it off in the jail or wherever they passed out, usually with little or none of their pay left. If the day-work cowboys were there at the same time, they found even more excitement. Sunday mornings for the ranch cowboys always meant the same thing, a long miserable ride in the hot sun back to the bunkhouse.

He found that dealing with Chance Patton required more skill than working with the rest of the hands. The big cowboy often delayed delivering the paperwork to the clerks and ignored him when he approached him about it. He'd ride into the cattle, when Heck needed to talk about something. Several times he'd thrown a rope over his head, pulling it tight, making him run behind his horse. Once he was knocked to the ground when he rode close to him.

Heck walked to the pens and motioned for him to come over. "Mister Chance, walk with me to the office."

"I'm busy right now," said Patton.

"Mister Chance, get down from that horse now and come with me to the office."

"I said I'm busy."

"You will come with me to the office now. If you don't you will be looking for another job," said Heck, staring directly into his eyes.

"You'd never do it."

He turned and began to walk toward the station. Patton watched for a minute then got down from his horse, tied it to the rail and followed.

He walked into the office and slammed the door behind him. "What's your problem little man?"

"It is a simple thing. You are going to do things my way. I am your supervisor. Do you understand me?"

"And if I don't?"

"You will be out of a job."

"What if I reached over there and grabbed you by your skinny little neck, what would you do then?"

Reaching behind the file cabinet, Heck pulled out the Winchester, levered a cartridge into the chamber and poked the muzzle firmly between his legs. "If you plan on working here any longer, you will do it my way. You will treat everyone here with respect. If you continue to go out of your way to aggravate me or the other workers, I will blow your huevos off ." When the big cowboy didn't respond right away, he pulled back the hammer with an audible click.

"Okay, put down the rifle, I was just messin' with you."

"This is the only time I will tell you this. You 'mess' with me one more time and you will lose your job and your huevos."

"Okay, little man, you're the boss, whatever you say," said Patton, backing up toward the door.

"From now on you will call me Heck and I will call you Chance. Do you understand that?"

Six foot-five-inch Chance Patton stood in front of him, his face flushed bright red — "I got it."

"And there is one more thing Chance . . ."

Patton glared down at him. "What is it? I've got work to do."

114

"Do not slam that door."

After the door closed behind Patton, Heck put the rifle behind the cabinet and went back to his paperwork.

*

In a few days Shan-Shan had the little house spotless. Despite his warnings, she left the house to shop for necessities, walking freely from the house to the few stores in town. After his first payday she had new cloth curtains with a bright red pattern and the blue and white fabric on the table. She built a pallet next to their bed for the baby and covered it with a new blanket.

Two new kerosene lamps, one for the kitchen and one for the sleeping area, brightened things up even more. She learned how to use the four-hole stove quickly, cutting the firewood to fit it by herself. She learned about the dampers and the ash catcher and had purchased a new pot and skillet that fit on it. She could now cook more than one dish at a time. Heck bought four each of spoons, forks, and knives for the table. "No more sticks for me," he teased. "I need a fork when I eat."

She always wore large, loose-fitting clothes in the old Chinese fashion and it hid her pregnancy. As she got closer to delivery time, it was getting harder to conceal. One day he took her hand and walked from the house to the small collection of businesses in town. "Our child is getting close; will he be here soon?"

Shan-Shan nodded, "Very soon."

"I have been thinking. I believe we should pick a new last name, like one that is common in America. We both have long and difficult sounding names. I want our child to have a good American name."

"Do you know a good American name?"

As they walked through the town, he stopped in front of a livery stable. "There, that is a good American name," said Heck, pointing to a sign above the entrance that said *Taylor Livery*. "That will be our new American last name: *Taylor*. We will be Shan-Shan and Heck Taylor — new Americans."

From that moment forward, they would be known as the Taylors. The sign over the front door of the station read:

AT&SF Railway, Magdalena, New Mexico
Heck Taylor - Station Master

Within a few weeks, Taylor had begun to earn the respect of his employees and the trust of his customers. Even after the rough start with Chance, things were running smoothly with the livestock end of the business. He would never fully trust him, but like Reeves told him before, he was very good at his job. He managed as many as two dozen cowboys. They move the cattle from pen to pen, checked brands, looked for sick cows, sorted them and moved them into the livestock cars.

Shan-Shan had met several women who were friendly and helpful. They had offered to assist her with the delivery and with the baby when it was time. Heck worked from sunrise to sundown or even later every day. When the time for the baby got close, three women were there to help. Walking through the door one evening, he was blocked by a stout, middle-aged Mexican woman with long gray hair. "Not right now. Go outside and wait, we will call you when the baby comes."

He walked around the house and the station for the next hour. He tried looking in the windows and found all the curtains closed. He walked back to the station and sat on the bench facing the tracks. Watching some pastores move their sheep from pen to pen. He realized just how skilled they were at working with their dogs, and how they kept the sheep together and moved them around on the commands from their masters.

He hadn't noticed the woman behind him until she tapped him on the shoulder. "You can come now. You have a fine handsome son."

He jumped up and sprinted toward the cabin, barely able to contain himself. Shan-Shan lay on the bed with the baby. "Heck, meet our son."

Heck sat on the bed and stroked his sons head gently. He kissed the baby and then kissed her. "I love you and our new baby. Now we are a real family."

"What will we name him?"

"I think I would like to name him Jose, for my friend that died in the mine in Zacatecas. "

"I think that would be good."

"He should have a middle name too, like most Americans."

"His middle name should be Lee, after my grandfather in China."

"Very good," said Heck. "He shall be Jose Lee Taylor."

Within a few days, everyone in Magdalena knew of the baby. Everyone who came and went at the station knew about the station master's new baby. Even Chance Patton gave him his congratulations. The ladies who helped midwife her also provided new bedding and clothes for the baby.

*

Magdalena had begun to grow and prosper, just as people had predicted. Within a few years it became the center for shipping livestock from Western New Mexico and Eastern Arizona. The silver and zinc mines were booming and several trains a day made trips to and from Socorro. The station had been enlarged and many more livestock pens had been added. Heck and Shan-Shan soon became two of the most well-liked people in the town.

Jose was soon joined by a brother named Andres. The Taylor boys were fast becoming as well-known as their father. They had the run of the town, and by the time they started grade school, they could already read and write and they had a good start on their numbers.

Shan-Shan decided when the children were born, they would have to study hard and learn as much as they could so they would fit in wherever they went. Both learned to read, write, and speak English and Spanish, and as they got older could speak fair Chinese. The rule was if you kept your studies and your chores up, you could go "exploring" as they called it. Jose was the obvious leader and Andres the follower of the pair.

One of the local ranches, the *Rafter JC*, about two miles west of town, allowed them to come and visit whenever they wanted. On weekends they would walk to the ranch and stay all day, often getting home after dark. They learned about horses and raising cattle on the open range. They helped around the ranch and with the gathering and branding.

The owner of the *Rafter JC,* an old settler named Sorenson, was friends with the family and kept them informed on the boys. "As long as the boys aren't in the way and if it is okay with you it is okay with me, but make them work," said Heck. "I don't have much for them to do at the station and I would like them to learn a trade so they will have a good way to earn a living."

By the time they were teenagers, both were skilled horsemen and good with cattle. The ranch gave them each a horse as payment for their work. Both boys stood about five-foot seven inches tall and had thick, wavy black hair. Jose was the leaner of the two and Andres, eighteen months younger, carried a little more weight and had a slightly rounder face. Like their father, they were considered very handsome.

The Taylor's were a close family and all four lived in the railroad house. They were exceptionally close to their mother, who had become a very popular figure in the town. She took care of her family and never said no to others in need. They had adopted Christianity and participated in all of the church activities, including a weekly Bible study. She taught local women to sew and cook and helped with midwife duties when needed. Classes for reading and writing were often held in her house for anyone who wanted to learn.

She loved to sew and make the boys clothes. "Heck, I would like a sewing machine so I can sew faster and for the ladies in town to use too. Sewing by hand is very slow, and it makes my hands sore. Can we afford one?"

Heck nodded. "I can order one from Socorro if you like, it will be here in a couple of days."

"I would like that. And please get needles and several colors of thread also.

"I will order it tomorrow."

She kissed him on the forehead. "Thank you, mi señor poco."

Several days later two cowboys delivered a crate to the house and set it where Shan-Shan directed. When they opened it, she thought it was just about the most beautiful thing she had ever seen. A beautiful brown wood cabinet with four drawers and black iron legs with the word SINGER built right into them. After looking it over for a few minutes the cowboys set the machine up for her.

"Thank you for your help, and tell Mister Chance thank you also."

She found all of the drawers full of dozens of colors of thread, needles, and ribbons. Opening the small book that came with it, she set to work learning to operate it.

Shan-Shan had grown from a pretty teenage girl into a strikingly beautiful woman. Even in the plain clothes she wore, she turned heads wherever she went. On special occasions she would wear colorful, traditional Chinese clothes and decorate the station and the house with paper dragons and lanterns. She cared for everyone in the small town as if they were her own family and everyone loved her just as much.

Heck's work took so much time, it made him unaware of all the attention that she received. At night they would lie in bed and talk softly about their day, often making love and falling asleep in each other's arms. As the boys got older, they became very protective of her. One or the other always accompanied her into town.

Jose announced at supper that he was taking a full-time job at the ranch and would be moving there in a few days. "What about you, Andres?" asked Heck. "Will you be leaving us too?"

"Soon father, but I would like to see some of the ranches up in the mountains before I decide."

Shan-Shan was quiet but her eyes showed her feelings. "I cannot believe it is finally time for my first son to leave home. I will miss him."

"I will still be close mother. I can come home often."

"We will be fine, just come when you can."

*

Magdalena continued to grow, and the railroad was the center of life for most businesses in town. Working close with the livestock and mining industry, Heck, working long hours every day, had turned a lonesome desert spur into a modern place for business. Shan-Shan was constantly busy with her church work and making clothes and teaching others how to do it. Heck bought her another sewing machine and the business of selling her clothes and teaching others kept her busy.

Her walks to town took her by several saloons, laundries and hotels. Dressed in her typical plain outfit, with her bag over her shoulder and her ponytail tucked inside her shirt, she paid no attention to those businesses as she walked.

On an early morning trip back home from the market, she walked by the saloons as usual. As she reached the house she realized there was someone standing behind her. A large, dirty hand reached around and clamped down on her mouth, pushing her through the door at the same time. Before she could scream the stranger hit her once, knocking her unconscious. Throwing her limp body violently onto the pallet he ripped off her clothing. After he brutalized her body, she began to wake up. Dragging her small body from the bed he hit her again. Looking down at the helpless figure on the floor, he picked up the fireplace poker and hit her on the head, over and over until she was unrecognizable.

The boys had been gone from home nearly two years when word reached Jose that his mother had been murdered. Racing into town hc pulled up at the house and burst through the door. His father sat at the table with his head down, sobbing softly. He put his arm around him and pulled him tight. "Father, tell me what happened."

Heck Taylor, the strongest man he had ever known, looked old and very fragile. His hair, now thin and gray, fell across his face and his hands trembled. He held Shan-Shan's blue wedding sash wrapped around one hand and the black cloth with the small gold coin in the other. "She is gone. A strange man killed her. People said he was a big man riding a tall bay with a black saddle. He hurt her terribly, then he killed her and left her body on the floor. He just rode away and left her covered in her own blood." He rocked gently back and forth with his father in his arms while he cried.

The whole town of Magdalena shut down for the funeral.

Jose put his arm around his brother. "Andres, you stay with father and I will talk with the sheriff about what to do next." Stopping at the station, he retrieved the Winchester and rode back into town. At the hardware store, he bought two boxes of .44/40 cartridges for the rifle and his own revolver. Walking into the office, he asked the sheriff what was being done to find the murderer.

"Right now, not very much. I have only the one deputy and he's out on another case. I wired the office in Socorro and gave him the details and the description, but that's all so far."

"This man murdered my mother. He has to be found."

"I understand Jose, I just don't have the help right now."

"Make me a deputy right now. I will find him."

"I can't do that. You couldn't be impartial. She was your mother . . ."

"Make me a deputy and I will find him legal. Do not make me a deputy and I will find him illegal — either way I will find him."

The sheriff nodded. "All right Jose. It's better to find him legal. But you need to bring him in whether he's dead or alive. We need to see the body to close the case, understood?"

"I understand. I will bring him in."

Handing him a badge that said *Socorro County Deputy Sheriff*, he gave him the paperwork and description of the killer. "We know his name is Garo Tompkins and he's well known as an armed robber, a rustler, and a killer. He's also wanted for a murder in Socorro. Jose, this is a really bad man, be very careful . . ."

His time on the ranch had transformed him into a lean, hardened cowboy, afraid of nothing. He wore a hat with a high crown and a deep crease in it. Made of black felt with a wide rolled brim, he wore it pulled down to his eyes. His pistol was on his right hip. A large knife was on his left side and the Winchester hung from the saddle. Tall boots with high heels made him look larger than he really was.

He had traded an old double-barreled shotgun for a good saddle made by Askew Saddlery out of Kansas City, his most prized possession. His horse, a smallish bay gelding, was one from his own remuda, the fastest one he had.

Untying his horse, he looked back at the sheriff. "I will find him and I will bring him back."

Andres watched over his father and took care of business at the station. Chance Patton had come to respect his boss and had become close friends with the family over the last few years and offered his help. He assigned a cowboy to stay in the station and keep a watch on it and the house until Heck was ready to come back to work.

Heck's loss was the entire town's loss. Women from the church came every day to cook and clean for him and grieve with him. After two weeks he could grieve no longer and went back to his everyday routine. The day after he returned, Red handed him a telegram from Jose. All it said was *I know where he is.*

*

Jose slowly picked his way through the trees. He'd been on horseback following a trail west for more than a week. In the wide dusty valley below him laid the town of Alma. A few buildings, a post office, and the usual variety of saloons and brothels were scattered out across the dirt. Years before, the town became known for a tragic massacre by the Apache Indians. Now it served a few remote ranches and mine operations.

After watching the saloon for most of a day, he decided he'd found the object of his search, Garo Tompkins. Age forty-one, six-foot tall and variously described as fat or heavy, and was wanted for two murders.

He found the Catron County Sheriff's office and it was empty. There was just enough space for a desk and a cell hardly large enough for two people. Leaving a note on the sheriff's desk introducing himself as a deputy, he explained his intentions. He pinned the badge on his coat and walked straight for the front door of the San Francisco Saloon carrying the Winchester in his hand.

Stepping through the door he quickly spotted Tompkins as the biggest man in the room. Leaning against the bar in conversation with the bartender, the man turned his head to see who came in.

Taking several more steps, he looked directly at the man. "Are you Garo Tompkins?"

"Who the hell are you to be askin'?"

"Socorro County Deputy Sheriff Jose Taylor. Are you Garo Tompkins?"

"And if I am, what do you plan on doin' about it?"

"I plan on arresting you or killing you for the murder of Shan-Shan Taylor. Whichever I have to do is okay."

Tompkins locked eyes with Jose and his hand began to move slowly across his belly toward a pistol in his waistband. "That skinny little Chinese woman? Shit boy, she was just another worthless goddamn chink. This country has way too many of them anyhow, nobody will miss her." When his hand touched the pistol's grip, the rifle went off with a deafening explosion echoing

123

through the room. The slug tore through his heart, blowing splinters of bone and blood across the back bar, the bullet lodging in the heavy wood frame. The man dropped to the floor in a pile. Before anyone could react, he had another shell in the chamber and the rifle pointed at the bartender.

Jose dropped a five-dollar gold piece on the bar and pushed it toward the bartender. "Here's what's going to happen next. You and your helper will put this guy over his horse, the big bay with the black saddle and tie him down. He's going back to Magdalena, so tie him tight. The money is for your help and for the mess."

Walking back into the sheriff's office he found it still empty. He added to the note he had left, "Done what I came to do."

*

After talking with his father and brother, he came to realize that he had found his place in life. A loner by nature, Jose had tended cattle and horses in some of the most remote places in the southwest. The job as deputy suited him perfectly. He rarely went to town and spent very little money. All of his pay and the extra money went directly into the bank in Magdalena and he seldom carried much cash on him. Once or twice a year, he went to the bank to check the balance. If the men he brought in were dead and had no obvious next of kin, the county sold the possessions and split the money with him.

His horses were his most important possessions and he hadn't yet found a woman who appealed to him. His job was tracking down wanted men and he was good at it. After bringing Garo Tompkins in over his saddle, the sheriff handed him a pair of posters and warrants for two men wanted in Socorro and El Paso.

Two weeks later he rode back into town driving a small wagon with one of the men shackled to the bed and the other dead in the back across a pile of saddles and other gear. The dead man had a single large hole in his chest. Two horses were tied to the back. Looking into the wagon, the sheriff asked if they gave him much trouble.

"No. Do you have another one for me?"

Within a few years, he was well known throughout New Mexico and Arizona. He always worked alone and his reputation as a lawman grew to legendary proportions. He once tracked a notorious Apache murderer named Indian Jake LaSalle for more than a month. When he finally tracked him down and killed him, he was covered in his own blood. He had been shot twice, once in the right side of his belly and once in his boot heel, injuring his foot slightly. The outlaw had been shot once through the heart. Over the years he had two horses shot out from under him and once made a legendary twenty-mile walk out of the desert after his horse had been killed.

Officials in Ciudad Juarez had requested his help several times to find Mexican criminals in the United States and several times he secretly went into Mexico and brought out American bandits. His appearance and his fluent Spanish allowed him to move easily in and out of Mexico unnoticed. As an outlaw, having Jose Taylor on your trail was the last thing you wanted to hear.

Often gone for weeks with his work, he decided he was ready to spend more time with his horses. Keeping his remuda at the Rafter JC ranch, he had little time to work with them. Visiting with his father and brother, he told them of his decision. "I decided to get a ranch where I can raise my horses and my family."

"Family? Do you have a wife? Or even a girlfriend?"

"I have a wife."

This news took Heck and Andres by surprise. It was something neither of them ever thought would happen. "Please tell us, why have we not heard of this?"

"Father, I am sorry that I have not spoken of this before. I have an Indian wife. Her name is Sara Song, she is Navajo. She had been taken from her people by two bad men, one of them was a wanted murderer I was looking for. They kept her captive for weeks. When I caught them, they were living in an old miners shack in the Zuni Mountains.

"What happened to the two men with her?" asked Andres.

"I brought them in. We have been together three years. We also have a son; his name is John."

"A wife and a son? Were you married in a Christian church?"

"No Father, we were married in an Indian ceremony."

"Will you at least baptize young John a Christian?"

"When I bring them down to Magdalena, we will have him baptized in your church."

"This is a lot for an old father to take in, to find out he has a daughter-in-law and a grandson that he never met. Where will you live?"

"I purchased a small ranch in the high mountains of Colorado, in a place called South Park. I have already moved my remuda there. Sara and John are there now. I would like this to be a place for all our family."

Leaning back in the chair, Heck rocked slowly back and forth. "I want to meet your family, but Shan-Shan is here, I could not leave her."

"And I am running the station now and could not leave such a good job," said Andres.

Looking at his father and brother made him sad. He knew this might be the last time he would ever see them. "Father, there is now a train that can take you all the way to a town in Colorado named Fairplay, it is very close to our ranch. Both of you can come for a visit anytime you want. When John grows a little more, we will come and see you."

Walking to the station the brothers stopped to look at the sign above the front door. "Father has always been proud of that sign," said Andres. "You know he started out as a worker in a silver mine in Mexico and left when he was fifteen years old for the United States."

"I remember the stories. Our father is a very good man; please take good care of him."

126

Trinidad

Clancy Tucker pulled the wagon up to the siding and waited his turn to back up to the chute. A stiff breeze swirled the coal dust across the tracks and covered the ground for hundreds of yards in every direction. His thick red hair and beard was often black by the end of the day.

When Clancy and Hattie Rose arrived in Colorado, he found work right away at one of the many coal mines in the foothills west of Trinidad Colorado. They lived in a small frame shack provided by the company. Most of the mines were owned and operated by the giant Colorado Fuel & Iron (CF&I), in Pueblo Colorado. The plant made iron from their own mines and used their own coal for fuel, selling the rest to outside customers like the railroads.

After the first week he announced to Hattie Rose that he had the best job in the place. Most men don't like working with the mules and horses and the broken-down old company wagons. They choose to work down in the mines. It pays a little better and they go down there for the money, but I get to see the sun and breathe better air up on top." He worked every hour of every day that the company would let him. When not working for the mine, he helped every coworker and neighbor in the area.

When he was home, Hattie would read to him about the old West. His favorite stories were about the Indians and the immigrants on the wagon trails. He loved the idea that they lived near the old Santa Fe Trail at the foot of the famous Raton Pass. When he did have a day off, they often went exploring, looking at the mountains and the places they read about.

Their daughter, Tess, was not interested in the stories like he and Hattie were. Always a restless strong-headed child, she rarely participated with the family, choosing to be alone. She had been caught stealing from the stores in town and had been locked up once for robbing a home. As she got older she would often be gone for days and weeks at a time. When she was seventeen years old, she left for the last time. Over the next few years they heard a few rumors about where she might be, but eventually those stopped coming.

Clancy had become a member of the United Mine Workers when he first started work in the coal fields. After a year of working as a teamster he was moved to Cokedale, the company operation where the coal was reduced to coke, a much more valuable product. He was soon the supervisor of teamsters and this enabled him to work even more hours. He was also able to keep his horses in the same pasture as the company horses. He had an agreement with his supervisor that they could use them when they needed a saddle horse in exchange for boarding them.

Although he had always loved physical labor and working outdoors suited him, he knew all was not well inside the mines. Conditions were notoriously dangerous and deaths and injuries were just part of the job. The United Mine Workers had been fighting for workers' rights and better conditions for years, and the company had been fighting just as hard against them.

In 1903 the workers struck for fourteen months. The Colorado National Guard was called in to stop it, and in the end, little was gained by either side. John D. Rockefeller, principal owner and one of the richest men in America was vehemently anti-union. Clancy was sure that one day soon the CF&I mines would explode into violence.

*

In September, the UMW called for a strike on the coalfields. The owners immediately kicked out more than twelve hundred people from their company owned houses. The union helped set up tent

128

cities large enough to accommodate the miners and their families and both sides dug in for a fight. The Tuckers found themselves in a twelve by fourteen canvas tent with a crude wood floor and a stove in one corner. Clancy chose to stay away from the main encampment and take one of the tents near Cokedale.

The camps lacked proper water and sanitation and the thin canvas did little to keep out the cold. He found scraps of wood and built a second wall around the lower part of tent. He covered the top with anything he could find, including pieces of canvas and animal hides. After finding an old buffalo robe, he used it for their bed cover.

That winter was considered one of the worst in Colorado history. Snow and ice blew down from the high country through the canyons and the rows of tents became natural windbreaks, piling up snow in enormous drifts. Temperatures dropped below zero for weeks at a time. Some tents were completely buried for days.

Clancy and the other men spent days digging out the camps and helping the residents with food and coal for their stoves stolen from the owners, a crime if caught by the company guards. By spring the residents of the camps were in terrible shape. People had died from starvation, exposure, and skirmishes with the guards. The union was running out of money and neither side had made enough concessions to bring the strike to a close.

Bitter feelings between the miners and the owners finally came to a head on a cold April morning, when the Colorado Militia tried to arrest the camp leader, a man named Louis Tikas. After heated arguments between the men, the militia set up a machine gun near the railroad tracks and opened fire. After getting reinforcements, they fired volley after volley through the camps and set fire to the tents.

In one of the bloodiest labor battles ever seen in America, dozens of people were killed. Under one burned-out tent, in a cellar dug for safety, four women and eleven children were found huddled together. Two women lived and two died. All eleven children died huddled together trying to escape the thick smoke.

By the end of September, the union had run out of money to support the camp and many new miners had come to replace them for the owners. These 'scabs', as the UAW workers called them, caused even more problems when the strikers tried to stop them. But the miners knew it was over and the strike was a lost cause. The story of eleven children and two women dying while hiding in a hole to escape the fires set by the Colorado Militia enraged the country. President Wilson, feeling the pressure, sent in federal troops to stop the bloodshed. In December, the strike was formally declared over.

"All this blood was spilled and so many people suffered so terribly, and for what?" asked Hattie.

"For a principal," said Clancy. "The strike was called for a principal. It was for a good cause, but everyone seemed to lose sight of that. The more we bowed our necks, the more hardheaded the owners became. They thought the miners would give up as soon as they got cold or hungry — they were wrong."

"What do you do now?"

"We go back to work."

*

After buying a small house in Trinidad with the money he saved from the coalfields, he quit the coal company and found work with the railroad on Raton Pass. "Tess, one day he might be hauling something and the next day he might be working on a water tank or a railcar. Daddy is as happy as I have ever seen him. We have a house of our own and he's home almost every night and has a place for his horses. We're both glad to be away from the coalfields. I think he is enjoying the time with the horses."

With the extra time, Clancy did jobs of all kinds around the town. On Sundays Hattie would read him new stories. They collected magazines and books and often read them over and over.

A library in town had a supply of old-fashioned dime-novels about cattle drives, Indians and outlaws, these were his favorites.

Laura Rose, the second daughter, was born on a bitter snowy night in the Trinidad house. Two neighbors assisted with the birth and the beautiful big-eyed, dark-haired child instantly became the love of her daddy's life. When Tess left, Laura was there to fill the emptiness in their life. Where Tess had been quiet and brooding, Laura was a noisy child, very outgoing and interested in everything around her. She was ahead of most of the children her age and schoolwork came easy. The Tucker family settled comfortably into life with their new daughter.

South Park

Jose Taylor snapped the reins and the horse strained hard into the collar. When the new fence wire was tight enough, John drove the staples into the new cedar corner post. It was the last repair needed for the new pasture. The recent purchase added a hundred-sixty acres of flat ground to the ranch. For now it would be extra pasture needed for the new horses, in time it would make good hay ground.

He led the horse into the barn and stripped her tack. Turning her out, he headed for the cabin. The bite of winter was in the air and the quakie trees had already lost their leaves. It was "see your words weather," as his mother, Sara Song, called it. At nineteen years old he was lean to the point of being skinny. His mother told him more than once he needed to eat more if he expected to be a cowboy.

The name John and his middle name Kenneth, came from a book about early cattle ranching. "He now had the first complete American name," said Jose. When he was ten, he informed them that he didn't like the name John Kenneth and wanted to know if he could change it to something else. Jose and Sara Song had a good laugh about this, and informed him that he was John Kenneth forever.

"What would you like to be called?" asked Sara Song.

"I think maybe J.K. It's much shorter and I don't know anyone else with a name like that."

"Well, I guess that's okay, J.K. it is," said Jose.

They chose the name *Taylor Land & Cattle* Company for the ranch and registered the *Rafter T* as their brand. Jose Lee Taylor, first generation American, cowboy, deputy sheriff, man-hunter and loner had retired his badge and hung it with his Winchester above the fireplace. All that remained of the deputy sheriff was his reputation. Jose Taylor, cattle rancher and horse breeder, had taken his place.

The ranch backed up against a pair of high mountains called the *Buffalo Peaks* and looked out over a mostly flat, wide-open grass prairie ringed by high mountain peaks called South Park. He and Sara Song had lived in a canvas tent for nearly a year while they built their first home. Made from local trees, it was twenty feet wide and twenty-five feet deep. In the center of one twenty-foot wall was a fireplace made of rocks gathered from the property. A ten-foot spruce log split in half was used for the mantle.

Running along the east side of the ranch, the middle fork of the South Platte River provided year-round fresh water. In the summer the cattle were moved into the high country to graze for six months. After a few years he'd managed to enlarge his property to six hundred and forty acres by purchasing two small farms in the area. He added a barn and a bunkhouse large enough for eight cowboys.

Jose liked it best when the cattle went to the high country, it gave him more time with his horses. Buying, selling, and raising horses was his real passion. J.K. had already taken over the cattle business and it was fine with him.

In April of 1917, President Wilson entered America into the war in Europe. In the middle of the Colorado Rockies, few people took much notice. It was hard enough to scratch out a living as it was. Losing any able-bodied men to the war was hard on the small farmers and ranchers, in some cases it cost them their land.

Now in charge of *Taylor Land & Cattle*, J.K. took on the task of drilling wells, building ponds and installing irrigation systems. He had a natural understanding of geography, water wells, weather and animals that few understood. When he acquired a new piece of ground, he immediately began to make improvements. New fences and a well were put in every large pasture not close to the river. As they became available, he purchased the foreclosures adding to the Taylor holdings. After one purchase Jose asked him what they had wanted for their land. "Eight-hundred dollars father, is that too much?"

"Give them a thousand. These people lost their son in France and now their land. Never let anyone say the Taylor family took advantage of people. Offer to help them move or anything else they need."

Jose took care of all the horse business for the ranch, spending his days working his horses and going to horse sales. He became a regular in Fairplay, the Park County seat, spending most of his time at the North Fork Saloon. Several hours a day, he sat in a corner booth buying and selling horses. If he did well that day, he always brought something home for Sara Song. "Sweets for my sweet," he said, touching her on the shoulder and handing her a small bag of hard candy.

"We made a profit today?"

Jose nodded. "We did, more than a hundred dollars from old Tom Frank up on the pass. He bought four yearlings."

"That's good. At least you don't have to be the one to break them, you are not getting any younger you know."

"I can still make love to my favorite Indian wife," he said, bending down to kiss her.

Pushing him away playfully she shook her finger at him. "I better be your *only* Indian wife old man, or no amount of candy will put you back in my bed."

Sara Song was a tiny slip of a woman, hardly over five feet tall, but her beautiful long hair and high cheekbones showed off the best of her Navaho heritage. When she was mad, she appeared much larger, always looking her adversary eye to eye and never backing down. "In case they give me too much grief, I always carry this," pulling a small pistol from her bag and showing it to a friend one day.

By now J.K. was a strapping six-foot cowboy who loved horses as much or more than his father. One day he disappeared from the ranch for several hours. Watching from horseback, Jose saw a swirl of dust coming down the road. As it got closer, he realized it was J.K. driving a truck.

"Father, what do you think? I just traded two steers plus ten dollars for it."

He shook his head and pushed his hat back. "What in hell's name would you do that for?"

"I'm thinking of buying a new stud from a ranch down in New Mexico. I'm going down to look at him tomorrow."

"Think that noisy old piece of junk will make it that far?"

"It's a Model T Ford with an extra heavy chassis and a Columbia body, the best truck there is, it will make it.'

"I will believe it when I see it . . . ."

"I'm leaving tomorrow. When I get there, I will look at all of his studs. You said yourself that we need to bring some new bloodlines into our remuda."

"We do, just pick a few good ones. How are you going to bring the horse back?"

"I made a horse hauler from an old car frame. I will pull it behind."

"You don't want to take a team and a wagon instead?" asked Jose.

"Father, trucks are the future as far as hauling things go. We have to get into the modern world someday."

"What about the train? That's the modern world."

"If I had a bunch of horses all at once, it might be good. But for just the one, I want to use the truck and the hauler."

*

The bar 7 ranch, outside of Raton, New Mexico was well known in the area for breeding strong fast horses. Many cowboys considered them to be some of the best all-around horses for ranch work and working cattle on the open range. They were also known for racing.

The Taylor Ranch had a track on their south pasture and every other weekend in the summer, local cowboys would come to show off their latest mounts and do a little gambling.

After a long, somewhat painful trip from the Colorado ranch to the New Mexico horse breeder's ranch, J.K. had his own doubts about the trucks of the modern world, but he would never admit it to Jose. Overheating and flat tires added at least half a day to the trip.

Dan Wilson greeted him at the barn. "Welcome to the Bar 7. I hear you're looking for a couple of good studs?"

"I am, but I need a particular one to start with. I want the fastest stud horse you have," said Taylor, as the rancher walked him through the stalls.

"This is the one you're looking for. He can outrun anything we have here."

"What's his name?"

"We call him King Red. Where you from?"

"South Park Colorado."

"How big's your remuda?"

"Right now we have about sixty head. We want to build that up to maybe a hundred over the next few years," said Taylor. "We raise and sell ranch horses and a few draft horses. Right now, I want to strengthen our racing stock."

"Red here will definitely help you out, he's a runner for sure. You said South Park, are you related to Jose Taylor, the famous lawman? I heard he lives up in that country."

"He's my father, he just raises horses and cattle now."

"Is it true that he spent weeks tracking down Jake LaSalle, the Apache killer?"

"It is, but he doesn't talk much about those days."

"I heard he spent nearly a month on the trail 'til he found him. Heard old Jake shot him in the foot and the belly before Jose sent him to meet his maker with a bullet from his Winchester, that right?"

"That's the story I grew up with. Now that he is getting older he walks with a noticeable limp. I think it's from the bullet to the heel. You ever get up to South Park come by and stop for a visit."

"Will do. Now what price did we decide on again?"

"A hundred dollars is what we said in the telegram."

"A hundred, huh? Well, seein' that it's for Jose Taylor, I'll take fifty. He put a bullet through the guy that killed my uncle down in Alma years ago. The family much appreciated it, so's it's the least I can do. Thank him for me, please."

"I'll tell him. I'd like to head out while I still have some light. Don't want to try the pass in the dark."

"Don't blame you there. Let's get him loaded so you can get movin'."

*

Pulling into the pronghorn roadhouse at the north end of Raton Pass, he walked into the bar and sat at a back table. An attractive young woman with thick wavy brown hair, large dark eyes and olive skin walked over and asked for his order. She waited impatiently for him to speak. Taking his hat off, he asked for a steak and a beer. "Do you have any potatoes?"

"No potatoes. We have a few canned turnips is all."

"Turnips? Are turnips popular here?"

"It's all we have. You want some or not?"

"Just the steak, and burn it, and the beer — no turnips. Oh, and a room for tonight please."

"A room's gonna cost you a dollar and fifty cents. The steak and beer is a dollar. You got that much?"

"I do."

"Pay first, then you get a room."

Placing three dollars on the table, he looked at her dark eyes. "Here's your money."

"I'll get your change."

"I don't care about the change, but I would like to know your name."

Turning her back on him, she walked to the register and got the change and a key. "Here's your change, the key is for room three." Turning her back on him again, she began to walk away. "My name is Laura Rose Tucker."

"Thank you Laura Rose . . ."

The bar was one of the oldest and most famous of the roadhouses scattered along the pass. It was dark and run down from years of the cowboys and teamsters coming and going over the pass and stopping for a beer or a meal. The bar was also a hangout for drunken cowboys wanting to pick fights with the miners or the sheep men. After a few drinks, the local coal miners were willing to fight just about anybody. On the rare occasion when an Indian came in, they set aside their distaste for each other and focused their attention on him. A sign above the bar said *No Indians Allowed.* It was all the reason the hard-drinking clientele needed to run him out.

Another sign that said *No Guns Allowed* was ignored by everyone. There was more than one bullet hole in the place, including one through the glass top of the cash register. The pretty brunette had been here for quite a few brawls and even helped to break some of them up. The bar owner often bragged about having the toughest barmaid in Colorado. "She's absolutely fearless when it comes to handling drunks, she's kicked more than one cowboy ass around here."

*

"I like the looks of this one," said Jose, checking the horse's feet. "Has he got a lot of good horses for sale?"

"It looks like he's got some good studs and some decent looking broodmares."

"What else did you see? Any draft horses?"

"No, he said he don't have much market for them anymore. Trucks are starting to eat into his business pretty bad. I did see a good-looking sorrel gelding I would like to have though."

"A gelding is fine, but we could use one more strong stud that has good cow sense. I want to work on our cow horse line."

"I'm going back next week to look at the others more closely."

"Why not bring several back on the train at once?"

"I just like to drive the truck. Father, the seller gave me a very good price on this one, a special half-price deal for you. He said to thank you. He also told me you shot the man that killed his brother. Somewhere in a New Mexico town called Alma. Did that really happen?"

Leaning against the fence rail the old man looked at him and nodded. "It is true. I was a deputy sheriff for Magdalena New Mexico and that was my job. That man was guilty of two murders, including your grandmother."

"What is it like father, to kill a man?"

"In my years as a deputy I never had any real feelings about killing someone. Those that did terrible things to other people needed someone to bring them in. I was that person. It was better for me to deal with them than to let them hurt more people."

"Did you feel that way about the man that killed grandmother?"

"No. That time was different. I was enraged to the point that I could not think properly. I let my feelings overtake my mind. When that man reached toward his gun, I shot him."

"He would have killed you if you didn't . . ."

"Maybe he would have, or maybe I acted too quickly through my anger. I don't know, but I never let my heart enter into my job again."

"What was grandmother like?"

"She was a slim, beautiful Chinese woman named Shan-Shan. Please tell the horse trader thank you for the good price on the horse, but when you go back you will pay him the full price. I was a deputy; it was my job. I think it is time for supper. Let's clean up and go inside now." He could see the pain still in his father's eyes when he talked about his mother.

*

He was on his fourth trip to New Mexico, stopping at the Pronghorn each time he came back. Whenever he came in, he took a table near the back. He always ordered a big steak burned and a beer. Each time Laura Rose served him with the same indifferent attitude, though he thought he could detect a softening of her hard line and once saw a bit of a smile.

It was Saturday night and the bar was packed with cowboys, miners, and working men of all types. The noise was nearly unbearable and the tobacco haze thick enough to chew. As he sat quietly, he watched the crowd get rowdier. Several cowboys at the bar were in a heated argument about horses and started shoving each other. When Laura Rose tried to break it up, one of them grabbed her by the arm, spun her around, and kissed her. She instantly punched him in the face and pushed away.

"Why you goddamn half-breed bitch. I'll show you what it's like to be with a real man . . ."

J.K. was up in an instant, stepping between them and punched the cowboy hard on the chin. The man dropped to the floor unconscious.

"Is there anyone else here that wants to talk bad to this lady?" J.K. asked the now quiet bar. "Is there anyone else here that has something to say to me?" The bar remained silent.

He looked at Laura Rose, nodded and walked back to the table. Laura Rose walked over and sat down across from him.

"The regular? Burned steak, beer and a room?"

"Yes, please."

"Would you like extra turnips with that steak sir?"

"Uh, no — no turnips . . ." Looking up at her he realized that she was smiling at him for the first time.

"One burned steak and one beer and no turnips, coming up. By the way, what's your name?"

It took him a moment to realize what was happening. This was his first serious conversation with her. "My name is J.K. Taylor. I raise cattle and horses."

"Well, thank you for defending my honor Mister Taylor. Nobody has ever done anything like that for me."

All he could do was nod. These were feelings he'd never experienced before. His face flushed and when she returned with the food, he could only stutter when he spoke. "Th-th-thank you, Ma'am," was all he could get out.

"My name is Laura Rose Tucker, but you already knew that."

"Yes," knowing that the less he spoke right now, the easier it would be for him.

"Don't be nervous, I don't bite I promise. I like you. You are the first man who ever treated me like a lady, instead of some cheap saloon girl," she said, touching his hand.

His face flushed even more. "Do you have a husband or a boyfriend Miss Tucker?"

"Why no Mister Taylor, I have neither."

"Do you own this roadhouse?"

"No, why do you ask?"

"Do you want to work here forever?"

"I hope not, but why all these questions? What's this all about?"

"If you marry me right now, I will take you to a beautiful ranch up in the mountains and we can raise cattle and horses and a bunch of kids and have a very good life."

Sliding a chair next to him, she stared at the good-looking young cowboy. Now it was her face that flushed. "You're serious, aren't you?"

"I am. I never met a woman like you before. You are smart, beautiful, and fearless, and I want to marry you and take you to my ranch . . ."

"Wait here, Mister Taylor. I'll be right back." Taking off her apron, she threw it on the bar. "Buck, I'm getting married, so I quit right now." Reaching in the register she took three dollars out and showed it to him. "This is what I have coming. Let's go Mister Taylor. We have to stop and see my daddy first, then we can get married and go to the ranch."

*

"Daddy, this is J. K. Taylor. He owns a big ranch in a place called South Park, way up in the mountains, we're getting married."

The giant man with the wild red hair and long beard stood up from his chair and looked down at him for a moment. "Getting married? What the hell makes you think you're good enough for my daughter?" Standing in front of this enormous man in ragged overalls and bare feet made him wonder if he had made the right decision.

"Can't you talk boy? How can you marry my daughter if you can't goddamn talk?"

"I can talk just fine sir, in English and Spanish both."

"Then goddamnit answer my question!"

"I am a hard worker and work on our family ranch. We have cattle and horses and a good house. I will take very good care of her. I promise you I will."

"You bet your skinny little ass you'll take good care of her. If not, I'll be coming to see you."

Laura Rose slipped her arm through her fathers to get his attention. "Daddy, you stop this right now. I already told you about him, remember? The cowboy from the bar that was nice to me?" This was news to J.K. He didn't think she'd even noticed him. "Tonight he rescued me from a drunken cowboy that was trying to grab me. He knocked him out with one punch. Don't worry, he's the one for me."

Clancy could see that his daughter was serious. "Hattie, you better come out here, this guy says he's gonna marry Laura Rose."

Hattie Rose walked into the room and straight to J.K. "Hello young man, what is your name?"

Removing his hat, he stepped forward. "I am J.K. Taylor, actually John Kenneth Taylor, from Park County Colorado. I want to marry Laura Rose and take her to my ranch."

"Laura Rose, do you want to marry Mister Taylor?"

"I do mother, very much."

She hugged her daughter and looked at Clancy, "Father, it looks like we better get to working on a wedding then."

"Well," said Clancy, "if you're sure then I'll go talk to Reverend Spencer in the morning. 'Till then Taylor, get the hell out of my house and come back tomorrow at noon. And for Christ sake clean up, you smell like horseshit."

J.K. found a room and a bathhouse in town. In the morning he went looking for a fresh shirt and a gift for Laura Rose. In the dry goods store he saw a gold ring in a glass case and asked to see it. When the storekeeper handed it to him, he could see a fine engraved flower on it. "It's a Columbine," said the man. J.K. asked how much.

"Fifteen dollars."

J.K. stared at the ring and the flower. He'd never spent so much money on something like this before. "That's a lot of money sir, I don't know if I can afford it or not."

"Tell me son," said the shopkeeper. "The one that you're buying this for, is she pretty?"

"She is very beautiful."

"A very beautiful woman should have a very beautiful ring, don't you agree?"

"I can afford ten dollars."

The shopkeeper looked at the ring once more then at J.K. "I can sell you this ring for twelve dollars, but that's the best I can do."

J.K. stuck out his hand. "We have a deal for twelve dollars."

At noon, J.K. knocked on the family's door. He had his hat in one hand and the ring wrapped in a small box in the other. When the door opened Hattie hugged him and took his hand, leading him inside. Slim, with her graying hair in a bun, she was still a very striking looking woman, her dark skin still smooth and her wide set eyes still beautiful.

"J.K., this is Reverend Spencer, the pastor from our church," said Hattie.

Spencer reached for his hand. "Good to meet you young man."

"Reverend, good to meet you too. Where is Laura Rose?"

"You'll see her in a few minutes," said Hattie. "Just sit here and I'll get her."

J.K. sat nervously waiting for his bride. When she walked out with her mother, he stood up quickly. He was sure his heart was beating loud enough for the other people in the room to hear. She wore a long dress with a red and white pattern that had been made by her mother and friends from the church. J.K. could now see red highlights flowing through her long brown hair. There were blue and white flowers laced throughout the curls. His heart raced even faster as Clancy and his bride approached.

Remembering the ring, he handed her the box to open. When she saw the ring, she broke into a huge smile and slid it onto her finger. Within a few minutes they were a married couple and the minister reminded them that could kiss if they would like.

As they left the house, Clancy pulled him aside. "I would like you to have a couple of our horses as a wedding gift. The next time you come through, you can pick them up."

"Thank you Mister Tucker, that is very nice of you."

"One more thing . . ."

"What's that?"

"Don't ever hurt her . . ."

*

They spent their first night in a small roadhouse in Pueblo. J.K. was overwhelmed with nerves. He had never been with a woman before and Laura Rose had only slightly more experience. He watched as she undressed and got in bed with him. She took his hand and placed it on her breast. "It's okay, we're married." They stayed up most of the night exploring each other's bodies and talking about their future and about how they met.

"If you told your father you liked me, why didn't you tell me?" he said, slowly caressing her.

"Every cowboy that walks into that place thinks he is a gift to all the women in the world. I didn't want any of them near me. They all smell like beer and tobacco and track horseshit all over the place. They're a disgusting lot and they all want to touch me and kiss me. I almost gave up on ever finding a good man. When you came in the first time, I assumed you were the same as them. After the third time I served you, I realized you were different. That's when I told Daddy about you. If you hadn't done something soon, I would have."

They drove through Colorado Springs and turned up the old Ute Pass road. The Model A slowed to a crawl until they reached the town of Woodland Park. After stopping for fuel and lunch, he opened the hauler to exercise the horse.

"Your truck does not go very fast up these hills, does it?" said Laura Rose.

"No, not very fast. My father said it would be better to take a team and wagon and tie on the horse. I think he was right. This truck is too slow and the ride is too bumpy."

"Then why not take the wagon like he suggested?"

J.K. shrugged his shoulders. "I wanted to show him my way would work. I did not want him to think I was wrong. I will put the others on the train."

"What's her name?" asked Laura Rose.

"It is not a her; his name is Lump, like a lump of coal."

"Why did you name him that?"

"I didn't. The man I bought him from did."

"That's not a very good name for a horse. It's kind of sad actually. Can you change it?"

"I can if I want. It's my horse."

"Would you name him Freeman?"

"Freeman? Why Freeman?"

"It's the name my great-great grandfather chose after he escaped from slavery. Today I feel like I have escaped to a new life, too."

After he loaded the horse, he gave her a hug. "I love you and I also feel like I'm starting a new life. From now on, he is officially called Freeman."

"J.K., does it bother you that my mother is black?"

"No. Why do you ask?"

"No reason."

*

Laura Rose could hardly believe she would be living in such a beautiful place. High mountain peaks and beautiful valleys surrounded the ranch. A cowboy on horseback greeted him when the truck came to a stop. "Who is this with you?" asked Jose.

"Father, this is my wife, Laura Rose."

"Your wife? When did this happen?"

"I met her several trips ago. She served me supper in the Pronghorn Roadhouse, do you know the place?"

"I have been there. So this time you decided to marry her?"

"After I went over the pass to get the horse, I decided I would stop and get her on the way back."

145

"Stop and get her? Had you already asked for her hand?"

"No father."

Jose looked puzzled. He tied up his horse and walked around to Laura Rose's side. Removing his hat, he looked at his new daughter-in law. "My name is Jose Taylor; I am his father. Is this true? My son didn't ask you if he could have your hand?"

"Yes, it's true. He stepped in when a drunken cowboy tried to grab me and he rescued me. Then he said come with me and we will get married."

"Did he at least ask your father for your hand?"

"He did. My father gave his blessing and got the preacher for us. He also asked that we take two of his horses as a wedding gift. One is a young stud and one is a mare. They're both from a line out of a very special horse named *River Man*. We can pick them up the next time we go back."

"Welcome to the Taylor family. Now I know why he chose to get the horses one at a time rather than put them all on the train at once. Please tell your father thank you for the horses. We will pick them up soon. Come with me and I will introduce you to his mother," said Jose, extending his hand and replacing his hat.

Within a few days, she felt like she had been part of the family forever. She quickly became Sara Song's friend and confidant. "It is so nice to have another woman in this wild collection of cowboys. It can get a little lonesome out here. It's all cowboys, horses, and cows. It's all they talk about and all they think about. Tomorrow we will go into Fairplay, and I will introduce you to my favorite store. We can get curtains for your room."

Jose and J.K. put a wall up in the bunkhouse, making a temporary bedroom. The cowboys were not using it this time of year and it gave them a little privacy. The original ranch house had been expanded twice before and they started right away on another bedroom for the newlywed couple.

Laura Rose quickly learned to love the outdoors and the horses and cattle. She loved the snowfalls of her first winter and soon became close to everyone in the family. After a couple of seasons, the ranch cowboys accepted her as a smart, hardworking cowgirl. She was the first one to get Jose to talk about his life as a lawman. She would sit in front of the fire for hours in the evenings and listen to his stories. In time she began to record them in her journal, along with her own family stories.

The depression had seen many of the family ranches and farms in Park County lost to foreclosure. J.K. had become so well-known and trusted that many of the ranch owners would turn to him before a bank foreclosure, offering him their land.

On occasion, J.K. was able to help them out of trouble so they could keep their ranch. Those that chose to sell were always paid above the going price and always offered any help they needed. The ranch had grown to several thousand acres, much of it in large connected pieces. The main body of the ranch had common boundaries with National Forest land and provided easy access to summer grazing.

By the time they settled into life on the ranch, the radio was full of war news. The Germans were invading countries all over Europe. Newspapers were full of stories and photographs of the battles. The outside world seldom affected South Park, but the war in Europe was now being talked about nearly as much as cows and horses.

Reading the week-old Rocky Mountain News, J.K. wondered why he hadn't received his notice from the Selective Service. Two men he knew had received theirs and were taken into the army. After supper he asked the family to talk with him about the war. He told them that he was going down to Denver and enlist in the army. "We owe this country father. Our family has done well here for many years and we should help if we can."

"No, I do not believe they need you to go to war," said Jose. "You will be the next Taylor to own this ranch."

Laura Rose sat quietly next to J.K. with fresh tears in her eyes. "We have talked about this, and if he feels this strongly, I think he should go."

"Mother, tell me what you think."

"You know that your father and I would like for you to stay here. But you are very young and I understand you feel the pull of adventure and patriotism. If you feel this strongly, we will not hold you back. We would be very proud of you."

The Split

J.K. never liked the big city. It always made him feel like a lost child. Finding the Selective Service office, he parked the truck and walked around the corner. The line snaked out the door and down the sidewalk for nearly a block. After an hour he stepped up to the counter. "Notice please," said the man without looking up.

"I don't have a notice, I never received one. But I did register and I'm ready to go."

The clerk finally looked up at the man standing at his counter. "Son, if the government wants you, they will let you know. Consider yourself lucky and go home."

"No sir, I came here to enlist in the United States Army."

The clerk called his supervisor over to the desk and explained the situation. "Young man, come with me."

Following him into the back room, the man directed him to sit next to his desk. "I have your file here Mister Taylor. I know that you have registered. The reason that you haven't been notified is that we use a lottery system. There are three hundred and sixty-five numbers assigned randomly to every day of the year. All American men between the ages of eighteen and forty-eight get their notice by what date their birthday is. If your birthday has a low number, you will be drawn early. A high number means that they may not even get to you."

"But I want to go."

"Like I said, you are in the system. The country will call when the time comes they need you."

"Can't I just enlist? I don't care about the number."

"Yes, you can, but let me ask you something. How long have you been wearing those glasses?"

"About a year or two."

"The lenses are very thick, take them off please." He removed the glasses and sat them on the desk.

"Read this please," said the clerk, handing him a piece of paper.

He could read the larger print of the title, but not the text. "I can't, but I do fine with my glasses."

"Mister Taylor, even if you do enlist, they won't take you. Your vision is just too poor. Please, just go home and take care of your family and do your job. Your country appreciates your effort, but it really is the best thing you can do."

*

For the next few months he tended to the ranch and worked with his horses. He was still bothered by the rejection, wondering why he couldn't wear his glasses in the army. "Teddy Roosevelt wore thick glasses and he was a soldier," he said, complaining to his father.

"What if you were in combat and you lost them or they got damaged? What would you do then? That is why they would rather take someone with better eyes."

"I suppose so, father, but I feel like I should be doing something to help."

"I think they did you a favor by sending you back home. Nobody needs to see all that killing and suffering. Perhaps you could be of help here by organizing the cattle ranchers in the park.

Many are having trouble making ends meet, and don't get treated well by the buyers because they are so small."

J.K. nodded, his mind already taking on the problem. Within a few days he had a plan and set out to visit every cattle operation in South Park. By the end of the week he had twenty-three ranchers willing to listen to his plan. Meeting in the school building in Fairplay, the largest town in sprawling Park County, they formed the South Park Cattleman's Association and Grazing Pool. By the end of the first meeting, twenty of the ranches plus the Taylor Ranch were on board.

Instead of the small outfits dealing with the buyers and the government war rules in place, they would throw in with Taylor and put their cows out on the national forest in the summer. Those who had only a few head and very little land needed to buy or grow additional feed, even in the summer. Taylor was able to run all the member's cows on the forest service land for the summer. He provided two cowboys to watch the cattle and move them when the grass began to run down in one area. The rest of the ranches provided extra cowboys to work the stock whenever they were needed.

When the cows were in the high country for the summer, the association, led by Taylor, began to look at ways to improve the irrigation systems in the valley. The small pastures that were crowded with cattle before could now be irrigated to grow more feed. The association drilled more wells for those that needed one and repaired or replaced fences as needed.

"This is very good," said J.K., after a ride through several ranches in the park. The summer grasses were high and the valley as beautiful as he'd ever seen. "This would be a good place to raise a new grandchild, don't you think father?"

"Laura Rose is expecting? That is wonderful news. Sara Song will have a young one to spoil."

"I am hoping for a son first, so we have someone to run the ranch when the time is right. Laura Rose says we need a boy and then a girl. We will see."

*

Laura Rose held the baby in her arms, wrapped in a soft red blanket. J.K. sat next to them. "You are the father. What would you like to name your son?"

"I would like to name him John Kenneth Taylor the Second and we shall call him John."

"A good strong name," said Laura Rose. "John Kenneth Taylor, meet your father J.K."

From the beginning, John had the run of the house, and by the time he could walk and talk he was the terror of the ranch. Wild and undisciplined, he was into everything he could reach. He'd broken lamps, dishes and even the kitchen window. His temper was always on display when he didn't get his way.

Ranch life took most of J.K.s time and Laura Rose had her hands full taking care of John the second. Within a few years the *Taylor Land & Cattle Co.* had expanded to be the largest ranch in the park. Taylor had purchased other property in the state and was continually growing the business.

Three years later, Laura Rose delivered Melissa Marie Taylor. As Missy became the new center of attention on the Taylor Ranch, young John became even wilder and more secretive. Although he could ride a horse as good as any adult, he really wanted nothing to do with ranching. When he wasn't in school, he was either 'exploring' as he called it, often being gone all day in the mountains, or stealing anything he could get his hands on. He would often get caught trying to trade or sell the items and ended up in trouble with the Park County Sheriff more than once. When the calving and branding work started, he was nowhere to be found.

When Missy was eight years-old she was a typical ranch girl. She loved all animals but really didn't understand the dangers of being close to the horses and cattle. She carried an old rag doll and wore cowboy boots with bright purple stitching on the top. Everyone working on the ranch knew to keep an eye out for her when she was around, because her natural curiosity often put her close to the stock.

In the spring, the branding in the park was at its busiest and the ranchers were getting prepared to form up the cattle pool. As the Taylors worked on the last batch of cattle, John took Missy's hand. "Let's go exploring, this is boring." Always happy for a little attention from her big brother, she followed him around the barn and started to climb up through the hills and rocks behind the ranch.

As the branding work began to wind down, Laura Rose tugged on J.K.'s sleeve. "Have you seen the kids? I don't know where either one of them is right now."

He shook his head and threw his reins over the fence. "Let's go for a walk."

After checking the bunkhouse and the barn they went back to the house. "I already looked here once," said Laura Rose.

In the house they went from room to room and opened every door. When they opened the door to John's room, it took them a moment to realize he was in the bed, completely under the blankets. John peeled back the cover and shook him. "Where is Missy?" When he got no response, he shook him harder. "John — where is Missy?"

"I don't know Dad; we were playing hide and seek and she went to hide. I looked for her, but I couldn't find her anywhere."

Grabbing his arm and pulling him out of bed, he lifted him off the ground. "John, listen to me. What happened to Missy?"

"I don't know, she just disappeared."

"You're lying to me, tell me what happened — now!"

"She went to hide and I never saw her again. It's the truth, I swear Dad, it's the truth."

"Don't you leave this house until I come back."

Laura Rose followed him outside as he headed for the barn. "J.K., I don't think he would lie about something like this."

"That boy lies about everything and you know it. Something happened up there and I'm going to find out what." At the barn he called together the branding crew and filled them in. Everyone there grabbed a horse and headed into the high country. For three days, the cowboys covered every inch of the ranch and thousands of acres of the forest land. By the time the search was called off, more than thirty men on horseback and on foot had scoured the forest and found nothing. The Park County Sheriff's Department had provided more men and the local ranchers and their wives took care of ranch business and fed the searchers.

J.K. rode alone up to the piece of rimrock overlooking the ranch. It was a small natural bench with a spectacular view of the ranch and South Park. The family often called it *Granddad's Bluff,* because Grandpa Jose Taylor had his ashes spread there. For the first time in his life, he broke down and cried. Not only was his beautiful daughter gone but it was the first time that he had a situation he could not control. His father had taught him that to be successful in business, there was no room for personal emotions. You must be in control of the situation at all times, or it would make you weak. Today he felt weak, he felt like a failure.

He stayed with Laura Rose for the next few months, but her tears were always close. By the first snowfall of the year she had begun to make her peace with it and move on. Nights in front of the fireplace with her books and memories and J.K. next to her was the best medicine she could ask for.

Young John stayed with his story and never said any more about the disappearance. By high school, he had little to do with the family and was even less interested in living in the mountains. He wanted to live in Denver. The ranch was too boring for him.

The same year John started sixth grade, J.K. had built two tables out of large wagon wheels for the living room, now called the long room. He cut a wood barrel in half for the bases and

153

placed the wheels on top. The space between the spokes were filled with family mementos and historical items and covered by thick glass. Jose Taylor's badge, spurs, and knife were there along with many local Indian artifacts. His Colt pistol was kept in a separate case in the office and his 1873 Winchester hung above the fireplace below a large print of the Charles M. Russell painting, 'Free Trapper', J.K'.s favorite.

A long, overstuffed leather couch faced the fireplace with overstuffed chairs on either end. Bookcases sagging under the weight of hundreds of books and mementos lined the walls on both sides of the fireplace. J.K. was a collector of the West. The house was as much a museum as a living space. Well-worn cowboy hats, chinks and leggings hung from the walls and rusty branding irons were stacked in every corner. There was nothing he loved more than to wheel and deal for a bargain on horses or western items.

By high school, John was a tall, good-looking young man who was a favorite of every girl in school. Impossibly thick black hair and dark eyes combined with a smooth deep voice made him look like an early movie idol. Those close to him knew his looks concealed a dark side. He was often mean and did whatever he wanted, regardless of who he hurt. He had a habit of stealing small things from his family and others, then selling it to anyone interested. His father found the Colt pistol missing one day and immediately went to John.

"Where is the old pistol that was in my office?"

"I don't know Dad; I didn't take it. I swear I didn't."

J.K.'s face flushed and his grip on his son's arm tightened. "You're lying just like always — where is the goddamn gun?"

"I don't have your piece of crap old gun," said John, twisting loose from his father's grip.

"If I find you had something to do with it, there will be hell to pay — you got it?"

"Yeah, I got it. Now leave me alone."

This was not the first time he'd been caught stealing from the house. Several items from the family had disappeared over the years. The most important was a small gold coin wrapped in a black cloth that had belonged to his grandfather. Like always, John denied everything. When the slave tag belonging to Laura Rose's great grandfather August came up missing from her dresser, they tore his room apart and found he had it hidden in his bedding.

"Do you know what that is?" demanded J.K. "Do you know how important that is to your mother and to this family?"

"It's just an old piece of scrap metal," said John.

For the first time Laura Rose told him the story of her family and why the "piece of old scrap metal" was so important to her.

John looked overwhelmed. "Are you saying you're black?"

"My mother was black and my father was white."

"You already know that you are part Mexican," said J.K. "But do you know that you are also part Chinese and part Indian?"

"Our name is Taylor. Where does that come from?"

"From a sign on a livery in Magdalena New Mexico. Great grandfather Heck wanted a European name so his family would appear to be more American."

"That's a bunch of crap — we are white! I've heard enough of this."

"Believe what you want son, it is what it is, you can't change it."

Driving to Fairplay for school the next morning, John stopped on the bridge over the Platte River and threw the ancient Colt into the water. "Screw you old man."

*

John Taylor's career at Colorado University was a series of parties, drinking, smoking pot, and chasing girls. He bragged about avoiding the draft with his deferment and how he was too smart to go to Vietnam. He graduated nearly last in his class with a business degree. When he was a Junior, he became infatuated

155

with a girl named Nancy Kay Miller. The harder he tried to get a date with her, the more she resisted. She thought he was good-looking but way too cocky and self-important for her taste. By the middle of her senior year, he had worn her down enough she finally agreed to "just one date."

She came from the small agricultural community of Rochelle, in Northern Illinois. She had five sisters and a brother, each about two years apart. The family were all considered to be quite attractive, but Nancy Kay was a truly beautiful young woman. Long thick black hair and perfect fair skin made her a very popular girl in school. She also had perfect grades and was in the University of Colorado for an engineering degree. In her first year, the school magazine did an article about the new freshman class of girls with top grades. Her picture was on the front page with the caption: "Nancy Kay Miller: Smart and Pretty . . ." Most guys that knew her would have agreed.

A few days after he graduated, J.K. called John to the ranch house. He had decided it was time to talk about the future of the ranch and his will. Walking up to the small bench on the hill above the ranch, he showed Laura Rose and John precisely where he wanted his ashes spread.

After this bit of drama, he took them to the long room of the ranch house. "Here's a copy of my will for everyone. I want to be sure that all of you know exactly what I'm doing and why I'm doing it." He read his copy out loud and paused a moment. "John, your mother and I have been all through this and we're in perfect agreement, you're not in it."

John, quickly getting red in the face, crumpled up his copy and threw it in the fireplace. "What the hell do you mean I'm not in it? I'm your only child. What are you going to do, take it with you?"

His father stared at him a minute and shook his head. "You are my only child; I can't begin to tell you how disappointed I am about that. You never cared about anything or anyone but yourself in your whole life.

If I die first, everything goes to your mother. Nothing on this ranch will ever have anything to do with you. From here on, you'll have to make it on your own."

By now John could hardly contain himself. Just as he was ready to erupt, his father stood up and stepped nose to nose with him. "Shut up and listen to me before you make it worse. I have decided to give you one more opportunity, and it's the last thing you will ever get from me."

"What kind of opportunity?"

His father handed him a thick manila envelope. "Here, take this and open it now."

The envelope contained a check for $50,000 and legal documents signing over ownership to him for a business in Denver. "It's a small property management company in Denver. It came to me as part of a larger real estate deal a few years ago. This is your inheritance, it's all you will ever get. The office is in downtown Denver, the address is on the document. I told them you're the new owner and you'll be there tomorrow."

Six weeks after college graduation, John Taylor and Nancy Miller were married and moved to Denver.

New Generations

J.K. watched the cattle head up the trail into the high country. A dozen cowboys moved them steadily into the forest, onto the summer range. For the next five months, the cattle pool would need fewer men to tend the herd. The members put two cowboys in the small forest service cabin in the high country and switched them out every two weeks.

They rode the national forest watching for problems and moving the cattle from area to area as the grass ran out. When they spotted a problem with a cow, they roped it and doctored it as needed. Branding was done over several days in the pen at the cabin by the ranchers in the association.

"Adriano, I think it will be a pretty good year. Lots of water and grass," said J.K.

"I agree boss, it looks very good for sure." Adriano Flores had been the Taylor Ranch foreman for years and was his most trusted man. Small and quiet, he was the best cowboy he'd ever had on the ranch. He lived in a second house, back against the trees, built in the late fifties just for the foreman and his family. The Taylor Land and Cattle Company had grown rapidly in the fifties and sixties and now had ranch holdings in several states. J.K. was often gone for business and he knew that Adriano would keep everything straight while he was gone.

*

John Taylor changed his new Denver property company's name to *Taylor Investments*. The business had six employees when his father gave it to him, and handled several large apartment buildings and two office buildings in downtown Denver.

Within a few years, he had grown the company to twice the original size. He and Nancy had also added three kids to the family tree. Chad and Thomas were two years apart and Kenny one year younger.

When the boys were old enough, they stayed at the South Park ranch for weeks at a time in the summer. J.K. and Laura Rose loved having them and taught them to ride and tend the stock. They also taught them about the land and the history of the area.

After a few summers, it was clear who liked the life and who didn't. Kenny hated everything about ranch life. He hated the animals, the dirt, and the lack of conveniences. Thomas loved visiting the ranch but preferred living in the city.

Chad was different. He was completely invested in the ranch, the cows, the history, and in particular the horses. He loved everything about life with horses. His grandfather could see from an early age that he had everything necessary to be a great cowboy and ranch boss. The more he challenged him, the harder he worked. A nearly perfect student in school, he fixed up an old pickup truck when he was sixteen so he could make the trip from Denver to the ranch on the weekends during the school year.

After high school, he decided to take time off to pursue the cowboy life. He moved into the bunkhouse as a day worker and for the next year he experienced every part of the business through every season. When he wasn't there, he was on the rodeo circuit riding broncs. After a year, he made his decision. He would attend Colorado State University and learn everything he could about the agriculture business.

Thomas and Kenny both went to college right out of high school and graduated with a bachelor's degree in business and went to work in their father's business. Thomas quickly became his father's right-hand man in the investment business and Kenny took care of the smaller property management side of things.

In his second year, Chad met a slim, pretty girl with beautiful eyes named Tamara. When he finally gathered up the courage to talk to her, he found out that she was two years older and set to graduate in the spring. "Where do you live Tamara?" was all he could think to say.

"Call me Tammy, please. I live in Collbran, Colorado. Do you know where that is?"

"I know Collbran, I've rodeo'd there before. It's a pretty place."

"You rodeo? What event?"

"I'm a bronc rider."

"Do you win much?

"I made three-hundred and fifty dollars there once."

"Well mister bronc rider, you want to tell me your name?"

"Uh, my name is Chad, Chad Taylor. I live in Park County, Colorado. Do you know where that is?"

"I know Fairplay, I rodeo'd there before. It's a pretty place too. Here's my name and phone number if you would like to call me."

"What event?"

"Barrel racing and team roping."

*

During the school year, they became inseparable, living together after just a few weeks. In the summer, he would go to her family ranch near Collbran or she would be in South Park helping with the gather or branding alongside of the men. After graduation she spent more time with him at school than at home.

Graduating with a master's degree in agriculture and a bachelors in American History, he returned to the ranch with Tammy as his fiancé. The wedding date was set for June twenty-eighth and the house was remodeled once again to accommodate another bedroom for the couple.

The party was the biggest, loudest, and wildest anyone in South Park could ever remember. There was bronc riding and storytelling and barrels of beer. The ceremony took place just after dark and was topped off by a fireworks display from Granddad's Bluff.

John and Nancy were there for the ceremony. They wished his son and new daughter-in-law the best and left. John hoped it would be the last time he ever had to come back to the ranch.

One evening after supper, J.K. asked Chad and Tammy to join them in the long room. "Grandma and I have something to talk to you about. We're not getting any younger and we've been working on a plan for the future of the ranch," he said, handing him a thick folder with the Rafter T brand on the cover. "Adriano has given notice that he is ready to retire. He's done one hell of a job managing this place for thirty-five years, but his health isn't that great any more. He and Maria bought a place in Fairplay and are retiring there."

"He'll really be missed Grandpa."

"Yes, he will. So, I need you to start running things as of right now."

He always thought this might happen someday, but he wasn't prepared to hear it so soon. "Grandpa, I don't know if this is something I can handle."

"Adriano and I both agree that you're ready and nobody in the family cares about this lifestyle like you do."

His face was flush and he was having trouble coming up with a response. "I'm not sure what to say here."

"Trust me, the right answer is yes. Besides, it's already a done deal. You are the new ranch foreman. That file folder will tell you everything you need to know about the Taylor Land and Cattle Company holdings. Next week we'll sit down in the office and start teaching you about that end of the business."

Tammy slid her arm through his and squeezed his hand.

"You can do it, everyone knows it."

"I'll do the best I can Grandpa, I can promise you that."

"As soon as Adriano and Maria are out of the foreman's house, it's yours. It hasn't been remodeled for years, so you and Tammy take it, gut it out, and do anything you want to it. You will need your own place for all those great-grand kids we're expecting.

"Chad, there's one more thing. When Grandma and I are gone, clear title to the ranch goes to you and only you. Your father and Kenny may never have as much as one percent of it. You understand what I'm saying?"

He'd always known that there was bad blood between them, but never knew the details. "I will follow your wishes to the letter, you know that."

His grandmother came over and hugged him. "We know this is the right thing and the right time. We've known it would be you since your first summer on the ranch."

J.K. stuck out his hand and squeezed his hand tightly. Then, in a gesture uncharacteristic of the old rancher, he embraced Chad. "We love you. We know you will make the family proud."

The first great-grandchild came almost exactly a year after they married. "Meet Robert Anthony Taylor, your first great-grandson," said Tammy handing him to Laura Rose. "We like the name Robert and Anthony is my father's name."

"What a beautiful boy, J.K., he looks just like you."

"Don't say that, the poor child will be cursed forever. Chad, I think he's almost ready to put on a horse, don't you?"

"It won't be long now Grandpa. Then comes the broncs."

"I don't want to hear any more about my new grandbaby on a horse," said Laura Rose. "You've got plenty of cowboys around here for that. Keep him close Tammy, or they will turn him into one of them, and you know what that's like."

"I do, I grew up around cowboys. Robert is going to be a lawyer or a doctor or something more civilized."

A year and a half later, the first girl in the Taylor family in many years was born. "It's just too beautiful of a name not to use it," said Chad. "We named her Sara Song Taylor, after Chad's great-grandfather's Indian wife." The whole family loved the idea and Sara Song soon became the topic of conversation all over the county. At the christening, so many people attended, the tiny Fairplay church decided to hold it outdoors to make room for everyone.

Two years later, Jeremy Albert Taylor was born during a bad spring thunderstorm. It was two in the morning and the electricity had been out all day. The only light in the house was a couple of kerosene lamps and the light from the fireplace. One particularly bad bolt of lightning hit so close that it shattered two big fir trees near the corral and they crashed across the fence. Six horses bolted through the opening and headed for the high country.

"Chad, let's go see what the damage is," said J.K.

They could barely see the corral let alone the damage. Torrents of icy cold water blown sideways by the wind beat steadily on them. The sting of sleet raised welts on their exposed skin. There were still several horses in the corral when they got there. "Let's get some ropes across the opening so we don't lose any more."

After covering the opening, they headed for the house, bent nearly to the ground to keep from being blown over. In the house they pulled off their hats and jackets and warmed themselves in front of the fire.

"I guess we know what we have to do tomorrow," said J.K.

"Cut firewood, fix fence and look for horses. Grandpa, this cowboy stuff is really glamorous, isn't it?"

The whole room broke out laughing at once, "I always thought so," said J.K. with a straight face.

"Chad, come hold your new son, Jeremy Albert."

Standing in front of the fireplace he held his new boy. "One day you can go fix the fence and find the horses. Then you can see just how exciting your birthday really was."

*

After the word of J.K.'s passing, a steady stream of South Park residents came by the ranch to pay their respect. Cowboys from all over the West and business people of all kinds sent their sentiments and flowers. The papers of every large city in Rocky Mountain West carried the obituary and many reprinted additional articles from past issues. The Denver Post did a story titled "South Park's Last legend." The turnout at the ranch was a steady stream for weeks. People brought food, cards and offers to help any way they could. Laura Rose graciously greeted all of them, listened to their stories about J.K. and all the things he had done for them. Sometimes she grieved with them.

Laura Rose and J.K. had moved to an apartment on the seventh floor of a remodeled building in downtown Denver. They had spent the last few winters there. They were both slowing down and the cold weather was taking its toll. The view of the city and the mountains was spectacular, and she was close to all the things she needed. It had large rooms and plenty of windows to see the mountains. After J.K. passed, Thomas set up a home nursing company to do a daily check on her and he came over several days a week to visit. Thomas always had a special relationship with her and had always referred to her as *Grandma Laura Rose.*

Thomas and his partner James had been together since college and recently bought a small photo printing business not far from downtown. Also nearby was John and Nancy's apartment. Laura Rose saw Nancy and talked to her on the phone often, but rarely heard anything from John.

An old back injury from a horse blow-up more than fifty years ago had her nearly incapacitated. Several surgeries and therapy had given her some relief from the pain but put her in a wheelchair while she was healing.

"Grandma Laura Rose, how you doing today?" Thomas bent down and gave her a kiss.

"I'm doing good for such an old lady, thank you."

"I want to talk with you about something that's happened at work."

"Sure, let's hear it, I'm always good for a listen."

"It's about dad. I should say about me and dad."

"Having a little trouble getting along?"

"More like irreconcilable differences. I have to be honest; I can't work for him any longer. He's just not a nice person. I'm sorry, I shouldn't have said that."

"Nonsense, you have to say what's on your mind and do what you think is right. Your father is not the easiest man to get along with, everyone knows that."

"I quit him today."

"Can you tell me what happened?"

"After working for him for all these years, it became obvious that he is unbelievably bigoted. He seems to hate everyone who's not white. He keeps all minorities out of his properties and won't do any business with them."

Laura Rose nodded. "I know he's always had a problem with blacks and Mexican people. Nothing we said or did when he was growing up could change him."

"I finally got him alone in his office and tried to reason with him. I wanted him to open up the business to minorities. He just blew up, saying no one tells him how to run his business, especially me. He said if I didn't like it here to get the hell out.

Grandma, I was so mad that I came out to him today. He hates gay people worse than the others. He screamed in my face calling me names I'll never repeat and told me I was disgusting and to get the hell out of his sight. He also said that I was no longer his son."

"Sweetheart, I'm so sorry you had to go through that. Let me tell you a story that might help you understand him a little better. When he was fourteen Grandpa caught him stealing items around the house. One thing he was caught with was something passed down from my Great-Grandfather August."

"What was it?"

"It was his slave badge. Do you know what a slave badge is?"

"I think so. Isn't it something the slaves wore so all owners knew who they belonged to?"

"That's right. My great-grandfather was a slave on a rice plantation. My mother was black, born to former slaves."

"Wow, what an interesting piece of history. Does the rest of the family know this?"

"Just your father. When I got the badge back, we sat him down and told him everything. He listened to us for a minute then exploded. He said he wasn't black or Mexican or anything else but white and didn't ever want to hear about it again. He always had a strange attitude about minorities. Even today he won't talk about it."

"Why didn't you tell anyone else in the family?"

"I really don't know, but it's time everyone learned about their family history. When I get through with all my tests and therapy, I will be in a wheelchair for a while. Then I'll go out to the ranch and we'll have a family meeting about the Taylor heritage. Grandpa J.K. has just as many interesting people on his side. What are you going to do now?"

"James and I will run the photo store together."

"How is Kenny doing? Does he get along with his dad all right?"

"I'm sure he'll be fine; he's already taken my place. He's also setting up dad's campaign organization. You knew he decided to run for president didn't you?"

"Your mom told me a little about it. After his time in the state house, I thought would have had his fill of politics, I guess not."

The High Country

The cattle pool had finished its spring calving and gathered all the members' cattle into the Taylor's large pasture. The trail up to the high country had been opened and cleared of fallen trees and debris two days before. The snow around the cabin door had been cleared and firewood laid in for the first shift.

By sunup the gate to the national forest was swung open and the pool riders started to push over nine hundred head onto the summer lease. They moved slowly through the muddy pasture onto the narrow trail. The steady bawling of the cattle would continue until they reached the summer pasture.

Pushing past Granddad's Bluff and up several miles of winding switchbacks, the country eventually opened up into a long string of wide flat meadows filled with lush grass and beaver ponds. At the back end of the meadow was the forest service cabin. Behind the meadows were the still snow-covered Buffalo Peaks. Alongside the cabin were two corrals, one for their extra horses and one for any cattle that needed watching.

As the summer progressed, the cowboys would move the herd from one area of the forest to another as the grass became available. Spending a two-week shift in the cabin was one of Chad's favorite things when he was a young cowboy learning the business. Being the boss didn't give him much chance to do it anymore, but he usually managed a day trip to the cabin once or twice a summer.

Encounters with bears and coyotes, as well as spectacular thunderstorms and the brilliant skies of the Milky Way were some of his favorite memories. He particularly loved the late spring snowstorms. One kept him in the cabin for five days straight with a Mexican cowboy who spoke no English and had a run-in with a skunk the first day of their shift.

Today he rode up with the herd alongside of Robert, who was taking his first shift as a pool rider. The trees dripped from last night's shower and early morning haze filled the low spots. Riding quietly, they reached the meadow and moved the cattle onto the grass. When they reached the cabin they saw several elk disappear into the trees. Tying up at the cabin they looked out at the scene in front of them.

"What do you think Robert?"

"I've never been up here this time of year. I think it's kind of sad that most people will never get to experience something like this."

"Robert, I know how much you want to stay on the ranch, but you know that mom and I want you to get a college education."

"I do. I just got my acceptance letter from Colorado State yesterday. I'm set for this fall. But in the summers, I want to live in the bunkhouse and take my turn up here. I'll also be home most weekends when I'm not rodeoing."

"The reason I brought it up is that I need a new foreman for the ranch. You need to get your college behind you and work a couple years and you will be ready for the job. Until then I need to set someone up for the job."

"I understand. I've got a lot of things to do before I'm ready for that."

"Good. I have to head back so I can get to work."

*

Chad asked one of his newest hands, Clete Bell, to join him for supper in the main house. "Can I get you anything to drink, another beer?"

"No thank you, a couple is my limit. Never was much of a drinker."

"Well, here's the deal Clete. I would like you to be my new ranch foreman, starting immediately."

It took him a moment to answer. "I'm not sure what to say. The offer is wonderful, but I don't know if I'm the right man for the job."

"I disagree Clete. You're just about the best cowboy I've ever seen, and I've seen a lot of them come and go. You're more in tune with the animals and the land and you're the best I've ever seen at anticipating problems." Draining the last of his beer, Chad pushed back in his chair and put his feet on the table. "You're definitely the man for the job. I'm spending more and more time on our other operations and I need someone here I can trust."

"It's not the ranch work, that's all I've been doing since I was a little kid. I'm just worried about screwing something up and letting you down is all."

"Clete, that's the last thing I'm worried about. I've screwed up a hundred times, hell, a thousand times, and we always work it out in the end."

"Well," said Bell hesitantly, "if you really trust me that much, I'll give it a try."

"Fantastic, Clete!" said Taylor, standing up and offering his hand to Bell. "Done deal. We'll get you moved into the foreman's house right away."

"Chad, there is one thing you probably don't know about."

"What's that?"

"Summer, my girlfriend, she lives in Fairplay. I was considering asking her to marry me, but couldn't really do it while I was living in the bunkhouse. Will this change things?"

"Congratulations Clete, that's great. Please invite her out and show her your new place. She's now part of our family too."

*

Thomas handed Laura Rose the tea and sat down next to her. "What's going on? On the phone you sounded so serious."

"Sweetheart, I finished this last round of therapy and I think it makes me feel a little better, particularly now that I am spending most of my days in the wheelchair. However, in the course of all my testing they found something else."

"What else?"

Taking a long sip of tea, she set the cup down and took his hand.

"Thomas, they found cancer . . ."

"Grandma, are they sure? You need another opinion. They're wrong about these things a lot of times," said Thomas, already wiping tears from his eyes.

"All the tests and second opinions have been done already. I waited until I was sure before I called you. You are the only one who knows, please keep it to yourself for now. I'll talk to Chad about moving me back to the ranch; I'd like to spend the rest of my time out there."

"Grandma, did the doctor recommend anything like radiation or chemotherapy?"

"He said it may add a little more time, but I have decided to have no further procedures done. I'm already miserable enough with the back pain. Twelve to eighteen months is their best estimate."

Laura Rose and Thomas spent the next few hours talking about family and about his father. "Grandma, I think there are some strange deals going on at dad's place. He was slowly cutting me out of parts of the business that I'd been doing. Then he formed this committee to study his chances of running for president. A lot of new faces were coming and going just before I left."

"I don't know what that's all about, but maybe your mom can help. Have you seen her since you left?"

He shook his head. "We're going to lunch tomorrow. I can't go to the house after the things he said to me."

*

John Taylor stepped to the center of the temporary stage. The street had been blocked off for the political rally and a large crowd had gathered to see the candidate in person. The Lee Greenwood song *"I'm Proud to Be an American"* pumped out of the giant speakers at full volume as the crowd waved and cheered.

With both hands in the air, he waved back at them, soaking up the adulation of the crowd, mostly party regulars that turned out for a look at the candidate. No one heard the crack of the rifle shot over the music and the cheering. Taylor dropped to the stage like a rock. It took nearly a minute for the security guards and the secret service to realize what just happened. Screaming for the paramedics, four men in dark suits surrounded the candidate with weapons drawn.

When the music ended and the crowd realized what had happened, they began to panic, looking for any kind of cover they could find. When the ambulance got to the emergency entrance, the press and hundreds of others surrounded the canopy looking for information. The police formed a barricade around the entrance holding back the crowd.

After two hours of emergency surgery, the doctor came out to address the public. "Mister Taylor has been wounded from a single shot from a high-power rifle. It missed his heart and spine by about three inches. The damage is extreme. He has been stabilized and is in critical condition."

The doctor answered a few more questions and said everything that could be done was being done. "He's in a coma right now, and only time will tell if he's going to respond to treatment."

Denver Sheriff Rulon Garcia spoke next. "We are currently conducting the most intense manhunt in the city's history. You have my word, we will find the shooter," said Garcia. "Right now, all we know is that he was shot from a high angle with a .30 caliber bullet, probably the most common rifle caliber in the world. We believe it was fired from a hunting style rifle. That's all I can tell you right now."

The family sat in the waiting room talking quietly. Chad just arrived from the ranch, still in his boots and sweat-stained cowboy hat. As he headed toward the family, two secret service agents stopped him. When they cleared him, he hugged his mother and sat down with his arm around her.

"Chad, can you keep everything going at the ranch?"

"Of course. You know he doesn't have anything to do with the ranch."

"Kenny, everything okay at the office? Any problems?"

"The office is fine Mom. I'm taking care of everything."

"I'm just trying to keep my mind on something else, anything else." Chad put his arm around his mother as she sobbed quietly.

*

Laura Rose listened quietly to the newscast, her grandson Thomas sitting next to her holding her hand. The news was about the attempted assassination of her son, John Taylor. They sat listening to the newscast as the details came out.

171

"Thomas, I've been talking with your mother and Chad. I think maybe it's time you went to see them. They could use all the support they can get right now."

"All right, I'll head over right away."

She had been putting off telling the rest of the family about the cancer and a few other things but knew it was time. "Tell them I need to see everyone together when the time is right. I'd go myself but it's so difficult with the wheelchair."

At the hospital he quickly found the intensive care waiting room and saw Chad's dirty black cowboy hat above the crowd. Next to him was his mother, her long hair pulled back from her still-beautiful face. The hospital provided a private waiting room for the family away from the news cameras.

As he walked toward his mother, she stood up and embraced him. Kenny sat in a single chair opposite the couch and didn't acknowledge him. Nothing had changed between them even after all these years. He told them that he had just come from Grandma Laura Rose's house and she would like all of them to meet at her apartment for a family meeting.

Kenny stood up and told everyone that he wouldn't be there. "I have to be at work. Besides, I have nothing to say to Grandma about anything."

"Kenny — just shut up!" said his mother. "For once just shut up and do what you're asked. I have spent a good share of my life listening to all of this family feuding crap and it's going to end right now — you hear me?" Everyone was surprised to hear this from her, normally a firm but quiet figure in the family.

He slumped back in the chair. "Okay, okay, I'll go! Now can I get back to work?" When it came to dealing with his mother, he always felt like he was eight years old again, instead of forty.

"Too many secrets for too long," said Nancy. "I told your father if he ran for public office again there was going to be trouble. I knew he wouldn't be able to go about his life as normal. I told him

172

people would be digging into our lives, dredging up old stuff he didn't want them to find, he just wouldn't listen."

*

Three days after the shooting, he was still unresponsive. The doctors knew it could take a long time for his body to heal. The blood loss had been serious. The paramedics had been close enough to get the blood flow stopped quickly or he would have died at the scene.

Laura Rose looked at her family. It was the first time in years that this many of them had been in the same room at one time. The only one missing was John.

"I have a couple of things I want to talk about tonight. I feel they are important enough that I needed all of you to hear this at the same time so there will be no misunderstanding. I have terminal cancer," said Laura Rose. "The doctors give me from twelve to eighteen months. Everything is conclusive. It's definitely terminal and I've chosen to take no additional treatments of any kind. I've also signed a DNR and made Thomas my executor."

The emotion began to flood Chad's face. He hugged her, unable to stop his tears. "Grandma, you're sure there's nothing else we can do?"

"I'm in pain every day from the back surgeries. I don't want to make life any more miserable than it already is. This is the right thing for me."

"Are you comfortable here, or would you rather move back to the ranch?"

"That's the next thing. I want to spend my last days on the ranch and I want my ashes spread with Grandpa's."

"We'll take care of everything."

"I know you will. After I get settled in there, I have a few more things to share with the family."

The Gather

It was nearly time for the fall gather. Chad was staying at the ranch and Clete would run the crew doing the gathering in the forest. Laura Rose was living at the ranch and watched from the porch as they passed by Granddad's Bluff and disappeared into the trees. The quakie trees were showing the first signs of fall and the sky was a spectacular deep blue. Kenny was the only one of the family missing at the table that morning. After a big breakfast, they all went to the long room and settled in with their coffee or tea.

"First, I want to talk about John's health," said Laura Rose. "It's been nearly two weeks and there's finally a little improvement. Nancy or I talk to the doctors daily. Although he's still in a coma, they seem to think that he's resting more comfortably. There is brain activity, but that's all I know right now." There had been several discussions about ending life support. Nancy and I have met privately with the doctors and decided it wasn't an option right now.

"Second, Sheriff Garcia, the FBI, and the Secret Service are working hard to find the shooter but haven't had any success yet. Nancy, Chad and I discussed it and decided to bring in a private investigator. His name is Jack Bannister and he runs Black Mule Investigations. He's also an old family friend. Some of you already know him. Be as helpful and open with him as you can. He has the run of the place."

"Third, I have a lot of family things I want to talk about. Now that I'm out here for good, I would like to get as many of us together as possible. It may take several evenings but I hope you can all make it."

"Grandma Laura Rose, I have an idea maybe you'd like," said Thomas. "I would like to record the conversations for the family. If it's okay with everyone else, I'll set up the recorder and James is a great photographer, he can photograph the family."

"That's a wonderful idea. Maybe you could expand that notion to include pictures of the ranch as well. Maybe we can start on Saturday, if we can get everyone here. Chad, do you think you can talk Kenny into coming?"

"Hard to say about him. We'll plan on Saturday, and I'll try and get him here."

*

With the cattle down from the high country and Robert back for the weekend, Tammy, Nancy and Sara Song prepared a huge meal for the family. Everyone was here except Kenny. Shortly after the meal, the family settled in the long room and a green Jaguar pulled up to the house. Kenny Taylor stepped out and headed toward the house, stopping long enough to hear the car lock click shut. Short, paunchy and shiny bald except for a small fringe of hair, he looked like a bookkeeper that rarely saw the sun. "Hello," he said as he walked into the long room.

"Grandson Kenneth, come here and give me a hug please," said Laura Rose. "I'm so happy you came. It's the first time that all of us have been in this room together in many years."

"Okay I'm here, but I'm not really sure why . . ."

"We're here to talk about Dad and Grandma wants to talk about our family history. Your dad is off life support and has nothing but a feeding tube in him, but his brain activity is looking much stronger."

Sara Song looked around the room, wondering why everyone was so quiet. "What's wrong with you guys? I'm glad that things are looking better for grandpa."

"You're right sweetheart," said Laura Rose. "I think we're all just worried."

"Okay. What else are we here for?" asked Kenny.

"By now everyone knows about my health troubles and that I'll be living here from now on. Thomas has offered to record what I can remember of our family history and James is going to do some photographs for us. And yes, Kenneth, we want you in the pictures too."

"Fine. I'll be in the pictures. Is that it?"

"John Kenneth Taylor, I told you to quit that crap. We all know you don't want to be here. You'll just have to tough it out," said Nancy.

"Okay fine, I'll just sit here quietly."

Robert and Jeremy sat on the couch with Sara Song in the middle. Long beautiful black hair, dark eyes, and flawless fair skin made her the striking image of her grandmother Nancy at eighteen. "Grandma, tell us more about the family. We really don't know too much, particularly on your side."

"Well sweetheart, that's as good a place as any to start this story. I'll begin as far back on my side as I can remember. My maternal great-grandfather was a slave named August, on a rice plantation near Charleston, South Carolina. The earliest reference I have is his date of purchase from a slave auction, August, 1851. It looks like he was about sixteen." Taking out a handkerchief, she unwrapped a small square piece of copper with a hole in one corner. "Pass this around please, it belonged to him."

When everyone had seen the tag, Sara handed it back to her. The room was quiet for a minute then everyone started talking at once. "Hold on everyone, I'll answer all your questions. Sara, you first."

"Grandma, are you saying that one of your ancestors was an African slave?"

"Sara, my mother, was black. Her name was Hattie Rose Freeman and my father was a big round, red-headed Irishman named Clancy Tyler Tucker."

"Wow, that's really cool," said Jeremy.

"Well, I'm not sure that everyone in the family will feel that way, but that's why I want to get it all down while I still have some memory left in this old head."

"What about his wife? Was she a slave too," asked Sara.

"Yes, her name was Sally. They escaped the rice farm about 1857 and made their way to a stop on the underground railroad walking only in the dark of night. They had help from three or four underground railroad families along the way."

"Where were they when they finally got free?"

"They landed about fifty miles west of Chicago. They agreed to stay and work as freed slaves for a farmer in the area. When they settled there, they added the last name Freedman. Eventually they dropped the 'd' and it became Freeman."

"Does dad know about this?" asked Kenny, suddenly paying attention.

"He's known since he was a kid, he just refuses to accept it. My grandfather Jacob and my mother Hattie were both born on that farm."

"That's a lot to take in. How come you never told us this before?"

"Well, I guess I thought everyone was busy with their own life and wasn't interested in the old stories."

"You have our interest now, that's for sure," said Sara. "How did your father meet your mother?"

"Oh gosh, are you really ready for all this?"

"Please don't stop now," said Jeremy. "I want to hear more."

"Believe it or not, my mother and father were born on that same farm. They played together as kids and grew up together."

"My father was a big red-headed white boy, my mother was a tiny black girl, and they grew up together. She was older than him, but he was her best friend since childhood. If you think that's interesting, my dad's grandfather was a confederate soldier in the Civil War."

"That's really a unique family tree for sure. What other neat stuff do you have in your history?"

"It's probably time for me to get ready for bed. How about this: those of you that would like to hear more, pick a time for the next history lesson. There's still lots more to talk about."

*

"Clete, jingle us up a couple of horses and let's ride up to the bluff," said Chad. "I have a project I'd like you to take a look at."

When they reached Granddad's Bluff, they walked to the edge and looked out at the view of the ranch. "Some of our family had their ashes scattered here over the years. Grandma Laura Rose has requested the same thing when it's her time. As you can see, once you get up here, it's kind of tight to walk out on the bluff. I'd like to remove this large slab of rock that's in the way."

The slab of granite leaned against another larger piece. "No problem boss. It might take a bit of powder to get it small enough to handle, but that's nothin'."

"Good. When it's all cleared away, I want to put a bench up here and maybe plant some quakies or flowers along the sides. It'll be a nice memorial for the family."

"Good as done, it's a pretty spot for sure."

"My Great-Grandfather thought so when he bought the place. He said the first time he looked down from here, he knew he was home."

"This is what the West is all about boss. Mountains, rivers and valleys all laid out like a picture postcard from the almighty himself."

"Pretty much the way I feel about it Clete, but I don't have a way with words like you do."

*

Saturday morning the family gathered in the long room to hear the latest about John and hear a little more of the family history. "Dad's still unconscious," said Nancy. "The doctors said that his color was looking much better and they're beginning to see a little

178

more eye movement. But they did find something else. The tests showed a large tumor in his head. It has apparently been there for a long time, probably since childhood. They've called in a specialist and the surgery to remove it will be noon tomorrow."

"The doctors aren't sure how much it will hurt his recovery, but it definitely has to come out," said Laura Rose. "We'll know more tomorrow night. For tonight we can talk a little more about the family if you'd like."

Robert and Jeremy sat on either end of the couch, leaving the middle the only place for Sara to sit. "Either of you touch me and I'll hurt you — got it?"

"Trust us, little sister, we would never do anything like that."

Dropping down on the couch, she looked at Chad. "Dad, if they touch me, I expect you to step in and save your only daughter."

"Save you from them? It seems to me that they were always the ones needing saving. Usually, it was you that had one or both of them crying."

"That's because they were jerks and they put horseshit on my pillow!"

The room exploded in laughter at the memory of the pillow incident. "We never put it on the pillow, we just put it inside," said Jeremy.

When the laughter died, everyone settled down and waited for grandma's next story. "Okay, where were we?" asked Laura Rose, wiping a tear from her eye. "After that, can anyone even remember?" After another hour, Laura Rose began to wear down. She was feeling weak, and Sara noticed a few small drops of blood on her tissue.

"I'm thinking it's past my bedtime. You let me know when you're ready for another history lesson."

*

The Taylor family stood up as the surgeon walked into the waiting room. "He came through the surgery very well. We removed a mass the size of a small orange from the left front side of his head.

It was attached to the skull outside of the dura tissue, and as it grew it pressed against the skull forcing it back into the brain. It was benign and we got all of it."

"You said it had been there a long time?" asked Nancy.

"We believe it's likely that it's been there since birth, possibly something genetic. The issue now is that if he does regain consciousness, we can't be sure just how this will affect his memory or personality. It's just something else we have to wait on."

*

The family sat in the long room for another Saturday night with Laura Rose. "Maybe something different tonight. How about a little history of grandpa's side of the family?"

"Sounds good to me," said Jeremy. "I know the rifle over the fireplace came from his side, but that's about all I know for sure."

"Robert, would you remove the painting from above the fireplace?" said Laura Rose. "Just set it here on the table please, face down. J.K. hung it up more than fifty years ago."

The back of the painting had names and dates written in several different inks and in pencil. "I nearly forgot about this. Grandpa liked to keep track of his family on here. Every time he learned something new, he wrote it down here."

Sara looked at the writing line by line. "This goes way back to someone named Heck Taylor and Shan-Shan Taylor . . ."

"Heck was a Mexican and Shan-Shan was Chinese. I seem to remember they lived in southern New Mexico somewhere. Their son, your great-great grandfather, Jose Lee Taylor, was a very famous lawman from New Mexico. I'm sure you can find him in the history books. The rifle belonged to him. His badge, spurs, and knife are in the wheel."

"Here he is!" said Thomas, "I found him on line! Jose Lee Taylor, Socorro County New Mexico Deputy Sheriff. There's a picture and everything," said Jeremy, holding up his phone for everyone to see. "There's several pages on him." The photograph showed a middle-aged Hispanic man with a large cowboy hat and high heeled boots sitting in a chair. He wore a badge on his left breast and spurs with large rowels. He was handsome, clean-shaven, and had a straightforward no-nonsense look on his face. Everyone crowded around his phone or looked it up on their own.

Laura Rose looked at the photograph on the screen. "That's really special Jeremy. It's the first time I ever saw a photograph of him. It's really wonderful to have a record like this. Jose Taylor is the one that bought the first piece of land for the ranch. He settled the exact spot that we're sitting on right now with his wife, Sara Song, your Navajo Indian ancestor. Their son, your Grandpa J.K., was about three or four when they moved here."

"Grandma, to have a history like this is really neat. We all have cowboys, Indians, blacks, whites, Chinese, English and Mexican and even an Irish confederate soldier in us!"

"And a lot of other stuff, I'm sure. This is just what Grandpa and I knew about. Sara, I'm appointing you the official keeper of the Charlie Russell family tree. You can add to it as the family grows."

"I think this is something I might write about for school, particularly about Jose and Sara Song," said Jeremy.

"That would make an interesting project, although some people may not believe you could have such a crazy mixed up family. I'm sitting here looking at the three of you, Sara, Robert, and Jeremy, the next generation of Taylors, and wondering where you might take the family tree next."

"Well, I know Robert will be here. He can't stay away from his horses and cows for more than a few days," said Chad.

"I'm going to become a lawyer specializing in western water law," said Sara. "I would like to practice right here on this ranch, if dad's good with it. I never really want to live anywhere else."

"What about you Jeremy?" asked Laura Rose.

"I've already decided to go to music school. I want to be a musician and a song writer. I might have to live in L.A. or Nashville, I'm not sure yet."

Chad checked the phone to see who was calling, it was Clete. "Hey boss, are you outside right now?"

"No, I'm in the house, what's up?"

Clete hesitated. "Well, it'd be easier if you came up here on the bluff. There's something you need to see."

"I'll be there as quick as I can."

Tying his horse off, he could see that the rock had been broke up into little pieces and Clete was waiting for him. "You find gold Clete?"

"Not exactly," he said, pointing to something behind the pile.

Chad stared at the spot for several minutes then sat down next to Clete. "Oh God, this has to be Grandma Laura Rose's daughter, Missy. She disappeared when she was about seven or eight." As he brushed away the debris, the small twisted skeleton began to appear. There were remnants of clothing still remaining, and a pair of cowboy boots with purple stitching. He could see that she had suffered a broken leg and a fractured skull.

"It looks like she took a bad fall from way up high and slipped down the crack between the rocks," said Clete. "She was just small enough to fit between them. It was likely covered with brush and pretty well concealed when she went in."

They sat silently for a while, looking at the remains. "Might be some kind of fate at work here Chad. Maybe the good lord meant for her to be found before Laura Rose passes."

"Maybe so. Will you cover her up for now and stay with her please. I'll go see Grandma and let you know what's next."

Chad and Tammy sat on either side of Laura Rose and he told her what Clete found. For a moment she was silent. Then the tears began to flow. "So it's over. After all these years of wondering, she was just playing hide-n-seek and fell?"

"That's what it looks like Grandma, a childhood accident."

"Chad, will you take care of her for now? When it's my time, I'd like to be cremated with her and have our ashes scattered from the bluff." She slumped into Tammy's arms crying softly on her shoulder.

*

After the discovery, Chad asked the family to meet at the ranch again to share the news. "The snow has already started. I hope Kenny will be here pretty soon or he could get hung up somewhere," said Laura Rose.

"I see his green car pulling in right now, it's hard to see it through the snow," said Jeremy. "The weather station says this could be a big one."
Walking into the long room, he found a spot by the fireplace.

"Hello everyone, I'm sorry I've been gone so much, but I'm here now. I hope you still consider me part of the family."

"You've always been part of our family. Nothing will ever change that," said Nancy. "We're always happy any time you can get here."

"Before we start anything else, there's something I want to tell you that no one else knew about," said Chad. "Kenny's been working closely with the Denver and Mesa County sheriff's and our detective Jack Bannister about dad's shooter. He may have seemed like kind of a jerk lately, but Jack didn't want anyone to know he was really undercover for fear it might have put his life in danger."

"Are you saying they caught the person that shot him?" asked Tammy.

"Right now they have a suspect in the Mesa County jail, I don't know any more details than that."

"That's wonderful news," said Laura Rose. "Maybe this will all be resolved soon. "Robert, could you give an old lady a lift to the bedroom please. I need to rest."

Picking her up in his arms, he took her to the bedroom and set her on the bed.

"I love you Robert. Don't we have the most wonderful family?"

"I love you too Grandma, and we really do have a wonderful family."

"Mom, I feel so bad. She doesn't weigh anything and I know she's reaching the end. I just don't know if I can deal with it," said Robert, wiping tears away.

His mother pulled him close, "It's okay sweetheart, we all feel the same way."

The headline in the Denver Post read:
"Suspect in John Taylor shooting in Custody"

John Taylor, Colorado native and presidential candidate, was shot while at a downtown political rally. "Mister Taylor is still comatose. He has been on a feeding tube only and is resting as comfortably as we can make him. The recent surgery to remove a tumor is healing well and it's now a wait and see situation as to whether he regains consciousness. "The sheriff's department has scheduled a press conference for 10:00 am tomorrow.

*

"I just came from the hospital. The doctors say Dad has begun to move around and make a few sounds. He appears to be waking up," said Chad. "Mom is getting the apartment ready for him to come home."

"It's so sad that grandma's not here to see what will happen," said Sara.

"It is sweetheart, but the idea of being with Missy again made her happy. Tomorrow we'll take the ashes up to the bluff."

Acknowledgements

Like always, writing has to be put out there to test readers you trust, a trial by fire if you will. This may be one of the hardest parts of the process. You have to invite your friends and other readers to scrutinize the manuscript and give you the honest, unadulterated, unvarnished truth. If you stink, they have to tell you — straight up. If you've done only a tolerable job, you need to hear that too. And if you did a great job — well, it could happen.

Nancy, my beautiful bride and best friend of more than 53 years, for keeping me around and keeping me straight. I promise I'll get those projects done soon.

Gary and Lenetta Haynes, for reading and re-reading 63,000 words over and over and giving me their honest feedback. They didn't always agree with me (or each other) but the help was invaluable.

Greg Wood, for reading all my books and still willing to read more — you are a trooper. Don't go anywhere, with the next one you get to watch survivor with me and get a pizza to go with it.

Bob Baker, my car guru and pal from way back. I know that we are getting too old for the B&B moving company, but we can still read and watch TV on our giant screens. My next one will be bigger than yours.

Bruce Florquist, a friend and wonderful reader and reviewer who volunteered to read my manuscript without knowing much about it or me — you are a brave soul, many thanks.

Liane Laroque, my editor and friend who always keeps me on the right track.

Don Kallaus, for all his help on my books over all the years. You keep on coming up with great ideas and beautiful work.

westernimages@msn.com

(719) 287-8063